BLASTER SQUAD #7

The Empire Strikes

By

Russ Crossley

53RD STREET PUBLISHING

Published by 53rd Street Publishing

Offices in Gibsons, B.C. Canada and Lincoln City Oregon, U.S.A

Blaster Squad #7
The Empire Strikes

Published by 53rd Street Publishing

Cover art ©3000ad

Cover designed by R. Edgewood
Cover design and layout © 2019 by 53rd Street Publishing
Print ISBN: 978-1-927621-68-4
Audio Book ISBN: 978-1-927621-69-1

53rd Street Publishing
Head office: Gibsons B.C. Canada
www.53rdstreetpublishing.com

OTHER BLASTER SQUAD TITLES

ACKNOWLEDGMENTS

Thank you to my Rita for supporting me as I wrote these stories over the past few years. They are a product of my life time love of science fiction.

For Rita, my dad and mom, and my friends who instilled in me a love of reading and of story. None of this would have been possible without their support and love.

INTRODUCTION

As readers of this series know this seventh book will end a saga of high adventure, spelling binding action, and thrilling cliffhangers in the long tradition of space opera. But I assure you, dear reader, Blaster Squad will return for further adventures. The squad is not done yet.

If you enjoy these Blaster Squad stories check out the short story, Mercenary Knights, available whenever you buy your ebooks.

Until next time strap on your blaster and get reading.

Russ Crossley
    Gibsons, B.C.
    August 2019

1

Unnamed planet
  Somewhere in the badlands
  Headquarters of the Master
  4154.9.3 Galactic

ASTY BONETES REGARDED the restrained Tribune Loa Marks through cold eyes from his seat behind the massive granite desk. The tribune was standing in the middle of the chamber shirtless, his heavily muscled body flexing as he strained against the plasti-steel chains anchoring his arms and legs to the floor of the rocky cave. The subdued lighting reflected off his chiseled torso. His purplish flesh was slick with sweat, though the air was cooler this far beneath the hot and humid surface of the arid, barren planet several kilometers above. Marks' gray eyes sent waves of arrogant contempt at Bonetes.

Bonetes would miss the tribune. He had a strength Asty appreciated and he had the enviable ability to carry out his duties virtually free of empathy. On Bonetes' orders, he'd recently cut off the head of one of the pirate captains as a warning to the others not to cross the Master or suffer the ultimate consequence.

Bonetes shook his head slowly as he withdrew the plasma pistol from his gun belt and laid it on the desk in front of him. He took his hand off the pistol and his eyes locked with Marks'.

The expression of abject hatred in Marks' eyes ebbed until all that remained was a reminder of the scowl wrinkling his forehead. Fear had replaced arrogance behind his eyes. Bonetes smiled to himself. He knew it wasn't fear of death—Marks had never feared death as long as Bonetes had known him—it was fear of Bonetes.

Marks knew Bonetes delighted in inflicting extreme fear and terrible suffering in his victims. It added to his mystic appearance of dominance and power to his followers. Of course, using the pistol like an ancient scalpel to surgically remove limbs while the victim was still alive was an excruciatingly painful way to increase terror and suffering before death. Marks had witnessed Bonetes inflict these sadistic tortures many times, sometimes over days, before finally erasing the victim's existence from the galaxy. The Master preferred maximum fear to a quick death.

"Emperor," began Marks, his harsh, dry voice barely above a whisper, "I'm not an agent of the Alliance. I'm loyal to the cause. To you."

Bonetes arched one dark eyebrow and his purplish skin darkened. He regarded Marks as it occurred to him the tribune might be telling the truth. Picking up the pistol, he disengaged the safety and fired a concentrated beam of super-heated energy at Marks' midsection.

Within a millisecond, all that remained was the tribune's final scream before he disappeared in a boiling mass of disruptive light, leaving behind the metallic scent of ozone as the only evidence he'd ever existed.

"I can't take a chance, there is too much at stake," Asty murmured in the silence. He arched one eyebrow. "At least I showed you the mercy of a quick death." Loyalty had to count for something.

What pleased him most was Marks had used Bonetes' soon-to-be-anointed title after he assumed the throne of the new Empire. To bring the Empire to fruition, his vast army and navy first had to defeat the Alliance. Nothing else mattered.

But before that happened, he still had one itch he needed to scratch. Blaster Squad needed to be eliminated. They had spoiled too many of his plans, and so far his minions had failed to kill them.

The Master smirked in the silence. Nick Justice and the rest of his band of mercenaries would die. Soon.

Bondar's Shuttle Tavern
  Calgary-Vancouver Megaplex
  North American Protectorate
  Earth
  Sol System
  4155.1.16 Galactic

LEANING FORWARD to rest his weight on his left elbow, Nick gazed down at the remaining amber-colored whiskey at the bottom of the glass on the scarred polished bar in front of him. Through his booze-impaired vision, he thought he saw Siren's reflection at the bottom as she used to be. Not as she was going to be. But hopefully as she might be again many years from now. Her death and resurrection by what he considered to be perverse science was all too much to grasp.

He was still thankful Gears had managed to download her mind into SIN, the System Information Network, before she died. The tech genius had then built a new artificial body to house her memories until her clone became old enough to accept her adult mind.

He froze and sucked back a shuddering sob, his eyes welling with tears. The Siren he knew was dead. The reality hit him deep in his gut and made his heart ache every time he thought about her.

The dimly lit bar had once been his refuge from his troubles during his early difficult days at the Alliance Naval Academy. The bar was always sparsely populated due to its location in an aging sector of old Seattle. The neighborhood was filled with the flotsam of Earth society. The great unbathed, as his grandfather used to say when Nick was a boy.

It didn't help that the floors of the ancient building creaked underfoot and the place stank of mold, booze, and burnt tobacco, though tobacco products had been outlawed for ten centuries. The ambiance appealed to Nick. The ancient tavern felt somehow dangerous and he assumed it was popular with outlaws of all kinds.

A hand placed on his shoulder from behind startled him from his ruminations. Instinctively his right hand dropped to his right hip where he usually wore his blaster, but the holster and the gun were missing. Then he remembered he'd left his pistol and gun belt in his room at the Fleabag Hotel over on First Avenue.

"We're here, you old space pirate," thundered a familiar, deep voice. One large hand slapped him hard on the back. He could smell them before he saw them. Rocky Bones and the Kid were behind him and they'd obviously been off on one of their sporting activities given the salty odors they radiated like a cloud.

"What is it this time, Bones?"

Bones erupted in a deep-throated chuckle. "Tell 'im, Kid."

Nick swung round in his chair to discover the sweat-streaked features of Bones and the Kid, dressed in identical black, one-piece, skintight jump suits, each with a yellow lightning bolt scrawled across the chest. He regarded the Kid with one eye closed so there wasn't more than one of him.

The Kid wore a silly grin on his handsome, youthful features. "Antigravity golf. We played for the championship of the system and won!"

Nick shrugged. "So what? It doesn't matter. Nothing matters."

He turned back to the bar, dropping his eyes once again to the half-empty glass of whiskey.

Bones grunted behind him. "Sir." Nick snorted derisively. "Captain," Bones said, starting again. "The simulacrum Gears and the SIN constructed has Siren's memories downloaded into its memory core. It'll look and sound exactly like Siren. It—I mean, she—will remember you...in fact, she'll remember all of us and all the things we did together. The bumps, the bruises, the ups, the downs—"

Nick swept the glass of whiskey off the bar, cutting off the weapons expert in midsentence, and spun round in his seat, his face contorted by rage. "But *it* won't be Siren! It'll be a damned robot, a simulation."

The Kid tried to place a comforting hand on Nick's shoulder but he shrugged it off, turning the seat toward the entrance to the bar. "Don't," Nick growled. "She was my friend. It isn't fair." His vision blurred and he realized he was crying. Tears stung his eyes and he blinked them away.

Looking fuzzy, as though viewed through a water glass, the short, wiry frame of Gears appeared before him as if from a fog. His ocular implants whirred in the quiet as his artificial eyes adjusted to the dimly lit interior of the old tavern. "We have a mission," said the tech genius simply.

"So?" mumbled Nick.

"Get it together, Captain," said Gears matter-of-factly, "Alliance Chair Lokfor Ust and Vice Chair Al-Mok Talon want to see us as soon as possible." Gears arched an eyebrow at Nick. "I think I'll ask them for a meet tomorrow morning. You need to sleep off the whiskey." His nose wrinkled. "You smell like a bankrupt distillery."

"Leave me alone," Nick snapped. "I'm working on my degree in drunkology." He chuckled at his joke. His expression abruptly changed to one of anger. We were wrong about Ust, ya know. She isn't the Master, ya know..."

"Bring him," Gears rolled his eyes then nodded to his two companions. Ust was furious when they accused her of being the megalomaniac trying to take over the galaxy. It had not gone well.

Bones and the Kid moved to either side of Nick, then grabbed him by his arms and lifted him off the barstool in one fluid motion.

"I'll get you all for this..." Nick's world disappeared into blackness as he passed out.

3

GSS Hunter
  Earth orbit
  Sol System
  4155.1.18 Galactic

IT HAD BEEN forty-eight hours since Bones, the Kid, and Gears had liberated him from Bondar's but his head still pounded. He had never been so drunk in his entire life. SIN said it was amazing he hadn't died of alcohol poisoning, and given the way he felt, he agreed with the AI. It was as if he'd been in hyper-sleep for five years, except he wasn't about to volunteer for one of those long-range exploration missions. He wasn't suicidal.

"Sir," came Gears voice over the comm unit next to his bunk. "Sorry to bother you, Captain," the tech genius continued not waiting for a response, "we have been cleared for departure. I estimate five days until we reach the optimum point in the system to engage the FTL drive."

Nick leaned forward on the bunk with his eyes closed. He held his throbbing head in his hands, willing the massive headache to go away. "Acknowledged," he said simply before slapping the comm button to cut the connection.

They couldn't engage the faster-than-light drive within a planetary system without the risk of creating an energy wave that would destroy moons and planets. So far the Master hadn't tried this strategy on any inhabited Alliance system. Nick speculated this was because he wanted his new empire intact. An Alliance filled with corpses wasn't much use to a megalomaniac who craved worshipers.

"Perhaps it's time to ask for some medical help," he muttered groggily. He could ask the SIN to provide medication to relieve the headache, but it was time to meet Siren 2.0. Siren had been a good field medic, so maybe her duplicate was too. He sat upright and sighed.

"SIN, contact Siren and tell her to come to my quarters. I need medical assistance."

"Anything serious, Captain?" asked the AI.

Nick rolled his eyes. "Just get her here."

"Yes, sir."

Nick stood and walked to the sink in his bathroom and turned on the cold-water tap. He splashed water on his face; the cool felt good on his skin. Grabbing the towel off the rack, he gingerly dabbed his cheeks and forehead to dry them, careful not to press too hard.

The buzzer at the door to his cabin signaled the arrival of his second-in-command—or at least a reasonable facsimile of his second-in-command.

"Enter," Nick said, his voice strained.

The door slid aside to admit her. She came in carrying a med kit. Nick thought he detected a familiar scent. *Tangerine, rose hip?* This had been Siren's favorite scent and this *robot* was wearing it. A knot of anger formed in his stomach.

It moved to stand near the bunk, waiting for him to acknowledge it. He paused briefly to study it from the bathroom before joining it bunk-side. The machine appeared the same height and body shape as the woman he'd known; its hair color and skin tone were the same. Its eyes were dark and looked as studious as Siren's had when she'd gazed upon him. The person he'd known had been an elegant, lean woman of remarkable intelligence, a highly skilled warrior who would kill without hesitation if the situation required it. Like Nick, Siren detested authority and would often argue with Nick over matters of authority over morality, though he was the titular head of Blaster Squad so he had the final word. Siren had once been described as the Alliance Navy brass' worst nightmare given her argumentative nature.

Now here stood a replica of the woman he'd known, his best friend, his second-in-command. Would this simulacrum be up to the task?

"How are you feeling, Nick?" said the android in a perfect simulation of Siren's voice. It even managed a perfect reflection of her sympathetic manner. It was spooky. It was using a hand scanner to check his vitals, its eyes serious, an occasional frown crinkling its forehead as it studied the readings.

"Ummm...not too good." Nick studied its eyes and saw nothing he recognized. "I have a massive headache. I took an analgesic a few hours ago..." His voice trailed off as he realized the faux Siren was holding a drug injector, ready to use it on him.

"Whoa, hold on," said Nick, stepping away from it. "I want a bottle of pills of some kind so I know what you're giving me. No injections. No way."

Siren arched an eyebrow. "Don't you trust me?"

Nick hesitated. "I don't know you..."

The faux Siren sighed and placed the injector back in its med kit. "Call me when you really want help." It turned to leave.

"Okay, Okay...yes, I trust you. Please get rid of this headache."

Siren's double shifted its gaze to lock eyes with him. Its narrow features betrayed no emotional cues like the real Siren would have in this situation. "You have an aneurism that is about to burst. Pills would do nothing to stop it from killing you."

Nick's eyes widened. "Give me the injection." He rolled up his right sleeve and held his arm out.

Siren shrugged, dropped her med kit on his bunk, and took out the injector. She reloaded the drug and injected him, accompanied by a hiss reminiscent of escaping air.

The throbbing in his head began to retreat immediately until it was gone as if it never existed. "I wasn't hung over?" Nick said, feeling better with each passing second.

"Oh, yes, Captain, you were hung over most assuredly, but hangovers don't kill you. Only aneurisms kill." There was no trace of humor in her tone or manner.

"Are you trying to be funny?"

She shrugged again. "Maybe a little."

The moment was broken when the comm signaled a message was incoming. Nick walked to the comm and stabbed the activation button. "Go ahead."

"The Chair has transmitted the coordinates for our destination," said Gears.

Nick hesitated. The Chair has been clear about this mission. The odds of survival were less than zero. They were hoping that, as a single vessel protected by a stealth shield, Blaster Squad would be able to infiltrate the Master's fleet to determine its size and as much as possible about the Master's plan of attack. They were then to break comm silence and transmit the information to Alliance Intelligence. If after this they were able to escape, they would re-join the Alliance fleet to continue the fight. Nick knew their survival was dependent on too many mighty big IFs.

Nick shifted his gaze to the replica of Siren and wondered if her memories really had been downloaded into its brain as Gears explained when he brought this thing aboard.

"Where are we headed?" Nick finally said.

"The badlands, of course." As Nick had suspected. *Into the unknown once again.* "But the real news is that the little Alliance Intelligence has been able to learn about the system we're headed for it that it is the most likely place Stormcrow ran to after the battle in the Gateway system."

"It's been almost a year since we lost track of him. Are they certain?"

"So they say," replied Gears, his tone suggesting he, too, doubted the information. The warlord had been elusive since their last encounter. And his AI had provided a false identity for the Master. Chair of the Alliance council, Lokfor Ust, AKA Lucille, was not the wannabe emperor of the galaxy. It had been an attempt to shake confidence in the Alliance command structure to make the Alliance easier to conquer.

A detailed examination by Alliance Security revealed that the times the Master's movements had been recorded did not align with the movements of the Chair. Nick was surprised when Chair Ust agreed to the examination so readily when he approached her with the evidence provided by Stormcrow's AI. She explained she needed the fleet and the council's complete confidence and loyalty to her if they were to prevail in the coming war. He agreed, impressed by her demeanor and confidence.

I may have been too hasty judging her, he concluded. His relationship with Edgar Whizzar had been special, so breaking in a new Alliance Chair was going to take time. He regretted not having instant rapport with Chair Ust; it felt strange and made him ill at ease.

But upon reflection, he decided the best way to remember his late friend was to bring the person or persons responsible for his assassination to justice. And true justice is often a dish best served frozen, as his grandfather used to say.

4

GSS Hunter
Somewhere in the Badlands
4155.6.25 Galactic

THEY HAD BEEN out of the FTL pods for five hours when the System Information Network reported there was an incoming signal.

Nick glowered at the left screen of the three screens in front of him in the copilot's station. "Go ahead, SIN," he grunted. The signal wasn't audial or visual, it was numeric. *A code of some kind,* he concluded. He studied the number sequence and tensed when he recognized the code and knew exactly what it meant.

"Bones, engage the stealth shields. Gears, evasive maneuvers, change course to 122.4 now!"

The *Hunter* lurched hard left and Nick was pressed into his flight chair, his strong hands gripping the chair arms as the anti-gravity system was stressed beyond its design limits. He heard Siren, Bones, and the Kid hit the flight deck behind him, accompanied by cries of pain, surprise, and a chorus of curses. No one had

had time to secure their seat straps because they had not expected an attack this far from the designated coordinates. They were at least two weeks from their destination at maximum sub-light speed.

Nick gritted his teeth against the mounting pressure on his chest and arms, and his muscles strained to stay seated in his chair. Perspiration dotted his arms and hands and beads of sweat ran down his forehead as he fought the sudden increase in gravity. He stole a quick glance at Gears and saw the tech genius had his shoulder straps secured and was struggling with the controls to maintain controlled flight after the sudden course change. Nick saw Gears was using the manual override controls rather than the automated system on his center touch screen.

After what seemed like an eternity, the pressure began to ease and Nick sucked in a deep breath of air. "SIN, report!"

"A magnetic plasma mine appeared in our flight path and has locked on to us. It's now matching our speed and following us along our new heading. The mine has its own propulsion system and was invisible to our navigation sensors until we changed course. It appears to have a stealth capability," reported the AI. "It became visible when we pierced its activation zone. If we hadn't changed course—"

"We'd be so much interstellar dust," Gears finished from the pilot seat, his voice thick with sarcasm. He shook his head dismissively.

Nick strapped himself into his chair before he asked, "Will it intercept us?"

"Its speed is increasing," said Gears.

"Will it intercept us?" Nick said more forcefully.

"Yes," said Gears.

"Will it pierce our shields?"

"No, sir, but it won't have to. My sensor scans reveal the amount of plasma contained in the device could take out half a continent. As advanced as they are, our shields won't be much good against that kind of power."

He glanced at Nick, his ocular implants whirring as he focused on Nick's eyes. "Unless..." He let his words trail off because they had had this argument before they made the FTL jump from the edge of the Sol system.

According to Gears, the *Hunter*'s faster-than-light drive systems had been upgraded such that they didn't need to use the pods anymore during the trip. They still had them as the fleet made its transition to this new light-speed process. Newly designed shielding around the ship made it possible to protect the crew against the effects of an FTL displacement wave. Nick found it hard to believe and was reluctant to skip the pods since, if it didn't work, they'd be dead.

"Dead crews can't complete missions," he explained to Gears.

He didn't mind death, but he preferred to die fighting—not because of some untested technology. The truth was this new design was just out of research and development and there hadn't been time to test it. The *Hunter* had been equipped with every possible innovation the Alliance Research and Development Division had, both on and off the drawing board. The ship had been rebuilt from the ground up and contained the most advanced propulsion and weapons systems in the history of the Alliance. They would need every advantage to complete this mission successfully.

Now it appeared the mission would end far sooner than expected when this mine caught up to them.

"When can we go to light speed?"

"Two minutes, sir," said Gears, not a trace of apprehension in his tone. He glanced at his sensor readouts. "The mine's speed is increasing exponentially and will make contact with our shields in three minutes."

"Bones, Siren, Kid, any ideas?"

"Other than I hurt all over," grunted Bones, "I don't have any."

"I say let's give it a go," the Kid said cheerily.

Nick rolled his eyes. He used his index finger to make a rolling sign to tell Gears to proceed.

"Siren?" Nick said to the Siren duplicate.

"I'm with you, Captain," she said sounding more like his old friend with each passing day. It might be eerie but she was growing on him.

"Okay, then, we're off." He shot a look at Gears. "Let's hit it, big guy. In for a dollar, in for a kopek." He grinned to himself as the collective groans filled the flight deck. *Thank you, Grandpa.*

5

GSS Hunter
  Somewhere in the Badlands
  4155.6.25 Galactic

NICK'S VISION cleared as they reentered normal space. The last few seconds—or was it hours?—were like those vague memories he experienced some times after waking from a vivid dream. He patted his arms and legs with the flat of his hands and was grateful to discover he seemed to be intact. The new FTL process worked.

"Where are we, Gears?" he said, his voice a little hoarse.

"Five million kilometers from our previous position," said the tech specialist, his voice sounding normal. Nick stole a glance at the pilot seat and saw Gears working his tri-screens, his fingers flying over the interface controls.

Nick shifted his gaze back to the screens in his station and swallowed hard. His mouth and throat were dry, but the FTL effects were miniscule in comparison to the old process.

He cleared his throat, then said over the internal comm, "How's everyone?"

"I could use a drink," piped up Bones.

"I'd second that," chimed in the Kid.

Nick chuckled. "Okay. Me too. SIN, materialize our preferred FTL electrolyte drinks at each of our stations," he instructed the AI. Immediately his favorite bottle of lemon-flavored water shimmered into existence in the cup holder on the arm of his chair.

He unscrewed the cap and took a big swig. The cool lemon water soothed his tongue as it flowed to the back of his throat. He swallowed and smiled to himself.

"Hey," complained Bones. "This isn't a drink. I meant a *real* drink."

Gears chuckled. "We *all* know what you meant, but we're on duty and have work to do, buddy."

The Kid snorted playfully.

Nick felt his forehead wrinkle as he realized Siren wasn't joining in on the usual good-natured banter of his crew. Such humorous teasing helped to ease tension before taking on a high-risk mission. "You okay, Siren?"

"Of course, sir. I was just running some system diagnostics after the unscheduled FTL jump. As far as I can tell, all ship systems are at optimum."

"Anyone get more information about that mine?" Nick puffed out his cheeks, trying to steady his mind. The effects of the FTL were minimal but there still were some. Obviously there were still a few bugs to be worked out to make the new system perfect.

Gears responded first. "The SIN and I managed to complete a full scan of the device and of the quadrant where we intercepted the mine before we jumped to light speed." Nick sensed Gears hesitation, meaning the news wasn't good.

"Go ahead, Gears, we have to know what we're facing."

"I could be wrong, sir, but a preliminary review of the scans suggests there are tens of thousands of identical magnetic mines along the heading to the coordinates provided by Alliance Intelligence."

Nick thought about the tech specialist's words for a few seconds. "Can we plot a different course to the target area?"

Gears nodded. "Yes, of course, but we also discovered these weapons were manufactured by a company called Galactic Inc."

Nick scowled at Gears when he stopped speaking, as if Nick should know who they were. "And?"

"According to a cross reference with intelligence data gathered recently about the Master, Galactic Inc. is a shell company for an illegal arms dealer who they think works for Asty Bonetes."

Nick froze and his skin became cool as blood drained from his cheeks. Asty Bonetes was the Master. He had joined the Alliance Council after the assassination of his father by persons unknown. The Kid had told him the story about how he almost killed Syd Bonetes—Asty's father—when he worked for Asia Call. The Kid claimed he backed out at the last minute when he realized he would have to murder innocent young children in the bargain.

Asty, in his position on the Council, had been responsible for alliance defense and security since his father's company supplied much of the military hardware used by the Alliance fleet.

This new revelation was bad news—very bad news. It meant all of the fleet's ships could be compromised, and that Asty was most likely responsible for his father's murder.

"Kid," he said to the younger man after casting his eyes over his right shoulder at the blond, muscular munitions expert in his seat behind him, "Come with me to my quarters." He shifted his gaze to Gears in the pilot's seat. "Keep us on this heading for now." As he rose from his copilot chair, he looked at Siren's double. "Siren, you're with me," he added.

The Kid joined him as Nick headed for the lift car at the far end of the flight deck. Siren left her station and followed behind them.

Nick sensed the rising mix of tension, uncertainty, and surprise surrounding him. No doubt due to the fact this was the first time he'd acknowledged the faux Siren as his second-in-command. And the first time he'd trusted her enough to join him in questioning a team member about an important element of the mission.

We all have to get used to new paradigms sometimes.

6

GSS Hunter
  Somewhere in the Badlands
  4155.6.25 Galactic

NICK STOOD beside the desk in his quarters with a glass of lemon water in his right hand. The Kid, seated in his visitor's chair, appeared calm, not the least bit concerned why he had been ordered here. Siren stood across the cabin by the door to the corridor, her expression solemn, with her arms crossed over her chest. She had strapped on her blaster. It hung heavy in the holster surrounding her narrow hips.

"Drink?" offered Nick.

"No, thank you, I'm fine, sir," replied the Kid, his brilliant blue eyes drifting between them.

Nick glanced at Siren and she shook her head slightly. He took a sip of the water; the cool liquid was pleasant against his lips. "Kid, I want to talk about the Bonetes job Asia Call assigned you before you joined the squad."

The Kid's brow wrinkled slightly. "I already told you..." His voice trailed off and Nick saw him stiffen in the chair. "I'm sorry, sir. If you want more than I have already told you, you'd need permission from the Alliance Chair. Those records are under seal and anyone opening them without the proper authority is subject to the death penalty." The explosives expert arched an eyebrow. "Surely you don't want me executed, do you, sir?"

Nick smirked. "No, of course not, Kid." He paused to shift his gaze momentarily to his second-in-command. She remained stoic. *I need to talk to her about backing up my glance messaging as the original Siren used to do. We were once called the salt-and-pepper of intimidation.* "But I need to know if the intelligence connection between Galactic Inc. and Syd Bonetes is true, and if that was the reason for the hit on Syd?"

The Kid's brow wrinkled and his eyes narrowed. "Why, sir?"

"If it's accurate—or even if it's mere speculation—it would explain a lot of what's been happening to us over the past few years." Nick look away at the painting of the waterfall on Telus II. The rainbow of colors surrounding the magnificent fall of rushing water always impressed him.

Siren crossed the room and stood over the Kid, her eyes serious. "The Master has attempted to put Blaster Squad out of business permanently several times, and I'm wondering why they think our little outfit is such a threat?"

The Kid's eyes looked quizzical until after a few seconds his cheeks drained of color and his eyes widened as the realization swept over him.

"Me?" he whispered. "They're trying to kill us because of me?"

Nick shared a look with Siren and they nodded simultaneously. "Kid, I think so, at least partially. I think the Master suspects you've been feeding us information about his operations once he discovered you were the hitter sent after his father."

The Kid shivered involuntarily. "Asia?"

Nick's chin sank to his chest. "I received a report two days before you found me in that bar that someone murdered her." His voice lowered to just above a whisper. "She's dead."

"And intelligence suspects Asty had his father killed or possibly that he did it himself," added Siren.

The Kid's lips pursed and his eyes burned with anger. His complexion darkened. "You mean he planned to kill his own father all along?"

Siren nodded her head slightly.

Suddenly the Kid's eyes changed to a look of horror. "How did Syd die?"

"His estate was destroyed in a massive series of explosions. His body, those of his household staff, the security team, and his family—including sixteen young children—were discovered in the wreckage."

The Kid hung his head, buried his face in his strong hands, and his muscular fame shook as he was overcome with emotion. "It's my fault..."

Nick nodded to Siren to back off. She moved away to re-take her place near the door. Nick placed one hand on the Kid's shoulder. "It's okay, Kid. But I do need to know a couple of important things." Nick paused to give the Kid time to gather his composure.

After a few seconds the Kid sat up straight and sucked in a deep breath. He used the palm of one hand to wipe away the tears from both cheeks. "What do you need to know? Anything for you, Nick."

Nick smiled to himself. As he suspected, the Kid wasn't working for anyone other than Blaster Squad. He'd put his life on the line so many times since joining the squad, Nick had long ago stopped doubting his loyalty.

Bones and he had become fast friends, and even Gears had worked his way from pure loathing to tolerating, which was a galactic leap for the tech genius who made all human and aliens alike work hard to earn his trust. It didn't help that the Kid's employer before joining Blaster Squad had been Asia Call, who Nick suspected was at the epicenter of this Master business. Gears had never trusted Asia, which as it had turned out could be right on the credits, as his grandfather used to say.

"I seem to recall you said something about after killing the security director of the Bonetes estate, you went after Syd and his son with blasters. Did you find them?"

The Kid shook his head. "There were too many guards who were on high alert after the internal sensor grid detected my gunfire. I barely made it out myself before a brigade of Syd's private army sealed off the estate."

Nick raised an eyebrow at Siren, who remained stoic. Syd Bonetes had had a private army? He'd never heard so much as a rumor about the arms dealer having a private army. He wasn't about to let on to the Kid he didn't know this information, but now he wished he could break comm silence and contact the Chair or Grand Admiral Schipp about this omission from his mission briefing.

"I don't recall anything about troopers' corpses being discovered in the wreckage, even in the intelligence briefings."

The Kid shook his head, his eyes closed. "I know. It seemed strange to me, too, at the time, and more so after you told me Syd and his family were assassinated."

"Sir," interjected Siren from the doorway, "I reviewed the records carefully and I can confirm the explosions took place two hours after the Kid was transported to Asia's ship in orbit."

The Kid froze and his gaze shifted to Siren as a slow frown came over his handsome features. "How did intelligence know I was there? I was undercover. No one knew I was there to assassinate Syd."

Siren arched an eyebrow. "As far as you know."

The Kid's eyes shot back to Nick and his brow wrinkled. "What is that supposed to mean?"

Nick grunted. "Never mind, Kid, I think we're done for now." The comm signaled he had an incoming message. "Go ahead," he said, not wanting to bother with the privacy manual activation.

"Captain," came Gears voice over the comm, "We have company."

Nick rolled his eyes. "Who is it this time?"

"I'm not sure. The vessel design and configuration are unknown in the Alliance or any of the known unaligned worlds."

Nick grunted. "Interesting. Is it transmitting any signals?"

"Nothing our comm recognizes as a signal or language in our database."

"Okay, I'll be on the flight deck in five." He closed the comm manually by tapping the button. "Come on, you two, let's get to the flight deck. This bears more scrutiny." The Kid nodded enthusiastically while Siren's features remained passive.

They soon entered the flight deck to find Gears busily reviewing incoming sensor data on the screens at his station and Bones rechecking weapons systems readiness.

Nick sank into the copilot's seat, his eyes traveling over the streaming data on his three screens. "Are our defensive screens at maximum?"

"Yes," said Gears, "including the stealth shield."

Nick turned his attention to the data on the screens in front of him. So far, the external sensors hadn't been able to penetrate the hull of the incoming vessel. It was four kilometers in length, one kilometer in width, and its velocity matched theirs. Its heading was parallel to their own, about two hundred thousand kilometers away. "SIN, have we tried to recalibrate the sensors to penetrate their hull? We need to know who we're dealing with."

"We have tried every setting we have and some we've never tried before, with no results," reported the AI. "It's almost like that ship is empty inside."

Nick scowled at Gears. "You mean there's no crew?"

Gears shook his head. "Not exactly, sir. SIN and I mean there is no discernable evidence of engines, crew, interior structure...it's as if it's a void beyond what registers on visible spectrum on the monitor."

Nick peered at the center of the three screens, and there against the star-strewn space was a vessel lit by navigation lights. He glanced at the telemetry data at the bottom of the screen and it showed the alien ship was moving. In fact, it was now closing on their position and its speed was steadily increasing the closer it got. *Navigation lights?*

Nick's heart froze and the tiny hairs on the back of his neck stood up. There was something very wrong about this picture. "Gears, what's our current speed?"

"Uh, point five FTL. Why?"

"If I'm read the data correctly, that alien ship is speeding up and is headed toward us on an intercept course."

"It will intersect our heading in fifteen point seven seconds," confirmed the SIN.

"Those aren't navigation lights," said Nick, almost shouting. "Those are holo projectors. Gears, take us to light speed now!" They had to get out of range immediately.

Without hesitation, Gears initiated the FTL drive and the *Hunter* lurched sharply to the left. The anti-gravity system was being once again strained to the maximum. Nick was pressed hard, back into his seat. His breath came in gasps; it was as if a heavy weight had been placed on his chest. He hoped the ship could handle the sudden acceleration.

The pressure lasted for several seconds until finally the gravity equalized and the pressure on Nick's body eased. "Everyone okay?" he asked. There was a distinct odor of smoke in the air, no doubt from overloaded circuits. Everyone replied in the affirmative but they were obviously struggling to fully regain their breath after the sudden unexpected FTL jump.

"SIN," Nick said, "what was that thing?"

"My readings show the holo projectors were masking an artificial wormhole." For the first time Nick could recall, the System Information Network sounded amazed and perplexed as it reported the results of its sensor scans.

"Gears, how is that possible?"

"It isn't...as far as I know." He too sounded stunned by this report.

"Well, I think, Gears, you and the SIN better analyze the sensor data in detail and come up with some sort of explanation. The Alliance needs to know if the Master has such a weapon, and how it works, or they're in real trouble." Nick was shaken to his core. He'd seen powerful weapons in his time, but harnessing an artificial wormhole required power far beyond known science, never mind controlling it—as this one appeared to be—was a threat to galactic peace beyond imagining in the wrong hands.

If such a weapon was turned on an Alliance world, they had no defense capable of stopping it. The targeting sensors of blaster or plasma cannons couldn't lock on to a wormhole. There was nothing solid for the sensors to detect. It'd be like trying to zap a cloud.

"Gears, tell me something." He paused and shifted in his seat to look at the tech genius, and to make sure he had everyone's attention, then continued. "That wormhole was moving—accelerating—and it changed course to intercept us. I've never heard of any space-born phenomena capable of these maneuvers. It penetrated our stealth shield, which is impossible. Any ideas?"

Gears' pale forehead wrinkled in thought. "There has to be someone or something controlling it," he said slowly, stating the obvious. He arched one eyebrow. "Somewhere in the sensor data must be a record of whatever was controlling the wormhole. SIN and I will include this in our analysis."

"Great. How long do you think it will take?" The wrinkles on

Gears forehead grew deeper. "Never mind. Just get me the information as soon as you can. Right now I need a course plotted to take us back to the target system, hopefully undetected."

Siren spoke before Gears did. "We were in stealth mode already, Captain, when the mine locked on."

"Well, then, we need a course bearing that in mind."

"Impossible," muttered Bones from the weapons station.

Nick smiled to himself. Bones was right of course, but they had a mission to complete; and if it meant going into a firefight, then so be it. He still had the uncomfortable feeling this entire mission was a trap to rid the universe of Blaster Squad.

This is gonna be fun.

7

GSS Hunter
 System 88899A
 In the Badlands
 4155.7.6 Galactic

IT HAD REQUIRED a series of stealth-shielded FTL jumps and some sub-light escapes, but they finally arrived at the outskirts of the system identified by the long-range AI surveillance drones as the system where Stormcrow had disappeared.

"What do we have on long-range sensors?" Nick asked after swallowing the sip of coffee he was drinking. The warm, milky fluid tasted good on his tongue. He set the cup in the holder on his seat arm.

"Uh," said Gears. "Siren, I need you to confirm my read on these results. I'm transferring the data to your station. You, too, SIN."

Nick momentarily considered interrupting his crew but decided against it. They were the best in the business, even the faux Siren was very good at what it did. In fact, it had almost made him think it was the real Sirenna Albright more than once over the past few weeks. Its responses to questions, orders, and situations even seemed exactly like the real Siren would have responded. He wasn't there quite yet in accepting it, but he was getting closer with each passing day. His resentment of the simulacrum had become razor thin.

After several moments, Gears—consulting in whispers with Siren and the SIN— finally reported his findings. "Sir, these readings are imperfect because the system ahead is surrounded by a dampening field. The upgrades during the refit to the *Hunter* did manage to break through the field—imperfectly, but enough to allow us some idea of what we're facing."

Nick wondered if the tech genius was going to get to the point.

Seeing Nick's reaction, Gears emitted a sigh, then continued. "According to these readings, there are in excess of fifteen thousand warships orbiting the three habitable worlds in the system, and each planet and moon closest to the star is covered with heavily armored facilities that not even the most powerful battlewagon in the Alliance fleet would be capable of penetrating."

"Stationary weapons facilities?" Nick whispered as the shock of the information washed over him.

Siren spoke before Gears could respond. "The planets and moons are armed with thousands of batteries of blaster and plasma cannons, and some energy weapons that the sensors are unable to determine their exact nature. The energy signatures of these weapons are similar to the energy source stolen from an experimental laboratory on Earth in 4140.2.3 Galactic."

Nick's cheeks grew cool and he shivered involuntarily. They had encountered this devastating energy before, but never in this magnitude. This situation was quickly going from bad to apocalyptic. "You said similar. How is it different?"

"According to the readings, the energy is more concentrated

than we've seen before, but we need to get closer to unscramble and obtain more detailed readings," explained Siren. "It's like looking at something familiar, yet different at the same time, as if through hazy cloud cover."

Nick smiled to himself. Her human-like observations were getting better. *Impressive*. "How close do we need to get?" he asked no one in particular.

"We need to study these weapons on-site. In person," responded the AI. "I believe you humanoids call it *up close and personal*."

Nick, Gears, and Bones chuckled while Siren snorted derisively in the most human mannerism yet.

"That's exactly what I was afraid you'd say," said Nick, his tone thick with sarcasm.

"Did I say something wrong, sir?"

"Not at all," said Nick with a sigh in his voice. "It's just that there is no doubt in any of our minds that we're going to have to run a gauntlet of fierce opposition, face death at every turn, and have to be the best we have ever been to survive the remainder of this mission."

"Yes, sir," replied the SIN. The AI actually paused as if considering its next words, then added, "In other words, Captain, just another day for Blaster Squad."

Nick nodded, then glanced at Gears, whose ocular implants whirred in the quiet as he continued to study the sensor data on his center screen. The AI was right: they had faced death many times and had always prevailed. Something about this mission, though, felt different. The first indicator was that the AI had just made an attempt at humor.

The magnetic stealth mines, the wormhole weapon, now these unknown, powerful energy weapons. Such weapons were not just to fight a war but also to create the maximum terror amongst an opponent's population, both military and civilian. This meant the emperor's goals were not only to conquer the worlds of the Alliance but also to subjugate the population and rule through fear.

Anger burned in the pit of Nick's stomach. To defeat the enemy forces, they would have to kill Asty Bonetes. The weapons merchant had crossed Nick's line in the galaxy and the only response Nick had left was to use whatever force necessary to disrupt this threat to the Alliance. And hopefully save trillions of lives in the process. His hope was they could achieve this without him and his team dying in the process.

8

GSS Hunter
  System 88899A
  High orbit Alliance planetary designation 88899A-3
  4155.7.14 Galactic

THUS FAR THEY had managed to evade the countless patrols roaming the system to arrive at the planet where Alliance Intelligence said Stormcrow had landed after his defeat by Blaster Squad. In low orbit were several hundred surveillance satellites, AI weapons platforms, all providing a security screen for a massive battlewagon, the design of which reminded Nick of Stormcrow's destroyed ship, the *Dark Storm*, only much larger.

Nick swallowed the mouthful of lemon-flavored water he has just taken in and wiped his mouth with the back of his free hand.

They'd beaten the odds so far, but he had a sinking feeling their good fortune was nearing its end.

"SIN, scan that vessel and narrow the location of Stormcrow as best you can." Nick smiled grimly to himself. If the AI had emotions, it would be insulted right now. AIs don't know what "best you can" means, or that it's an insult.

During the perilous journey past the numerous pirate ship patrols and automated security sensor platforms dotting the system, they had agreed on a plan. They would divert all extra power, including the power for the weapons systems, to the stealth shield to hopefully ensure they wouldn't be detected. Gears reported the defenses' design was indicative of a style meant to detect fleets of ships nearing the system. A single ship with a viable stealth shield might be able to elude detection. With their weapons disabled this would be risky, but they had little choice other than to try.

Given the vast scope of the Master's operation—and the never before weapons technology being deployed—Nick realized it must have cost Bonetes trillions of credits to pull this off. He wasn't just insane, he was deadly serious and more dangerous than even Nick could have imagined.

Upon arrival in orbit and in range of Stormcrow's battlewagon, the plan was to use the materializer to kidnap Stormcrow, then compel him to reveal the location of Asty Bonetes. Once they knew the location of the would-be emperor, they would take him out by whatever means available. This would, of course, require them to lower the stealth shield and become visible to every enemy ship and gun battery in the system.

When they revealed their position, the odds of survival were somewhere between slim and none, but that was the mission, and as far as Nick and the squad were concerned, the ultimate sacrifice was worth the lives of billions and billions of the human and nonhuman races that populated the vast expanse of the galaxy.

Nick hoped the enemy would be caught off guard by a single ship managing to bypass their security so that it'd buy them time to capture Stormcrow in the confusion. Once they had the rogue warlord in their hands, they would use him as a bargaining chip to hold off the enemy forces. They would then escape with Storm-crow as a shield until they found the location of Bonetes. Once that happened, Nick wasn't sure what they'd do with Percy next.

Of course, then they would have to deal with the massive enemy fleet and the thousands of troops scattered across the worlds and moons in the system, and those stationed on the instal-lations in orbit around those same moons and planets, tracking them and vaporizing them before they could escape. Frankly, the entire operation seemed impossibly insane.

Something odd on Nick's right screen caught his attention. "Gears, I'm reading some weapons signatures within the troop concentrations on the planet and its moon."

"I'm not sure, Captain."

"I might be able to explain," offered Bones. "The signatures are reminiscent of many different types of energy weapons. Some very old designs, some very new. There are many different types and classes of weapons. From old style one-shot blasters to the most recent issue Alliance plasma weapons, and everything in between."

Nick thought for a few seconds. His mouth dried, so he raised his glass and let the cool lemon water moisten his lips and throat. "I suspect this is true of the entire army we are facing," he said.

"What does that mean?" asked the Kid.

"It means the Master is not quite as invincible as we believed, but his army is an irregular collection of pirates, mercenaries, and the scum of the badlands. It's unlikely they'll be able to take orders very well or be as disciplined as the Alliance Navy when it comes to a straight-up fight."

"That doesn't make much sense," said Siren, the confusion evident in her tone.

"Unless it's a trap," said Gears.

"SIN, initiate emergency FTL jump!" shouted Nick.

"Sir, I'm tracking multiple weapons' targeting systems that

have locked on to us. Somehow they've been able to penetrate our —" Gears words disappeared as Nick was assaulted by a sudden increase in g-forces pressing him into his seat. His breath caught in his throat and his lungs began to burn. His heart pounded in his chest and he wondered if this was what it felt like to die.

9

GSS Hunter
  Somewhere in uncharted space
  Date unknown

NICK'S EYES FLUTTERED OPEN. The metallic taste of blood coated his tongue and mouth. His thoughts were jumbled as if he'd woken from a long sleep after a binge night on the town. The last thing he recalled was ordering the SIN to initiate an emergency FTL jump. "Ohhh," he groaned, "my head hurts."

"We all hurt," said the groggy voice of Bones.

"I'm with him," said the Kid.

"Gears, where are we?" Nick asked the tech genius sitting to his right in the pilot's seat.

"Give me a few minutes," replied Gears, his voice trembling. "Our engines and sensor systems are off-line. We're drifting." He sighed. "It's a wonder anti-gravity and life support are still functioning." He stabbed an index finger at the center screen in front of him, his frustration evident. "Even the System Information Network is off-line."

"My weapons are dead," said Bones, his voice angry.

"Siren?" Nick asked his second-in-command, "any ideas?"

"I have our short-range sensors back..." Her voice trailed off. "Huh. Sir, there is an unidentified vessel a kilometer off our port side."

If this unknown ship was part of the Master's fleet, without engines or weapons this mission was over before it began. Their luck had just run out.

"We're receiving a comm message. Voice only," said a perplexed Gear. Nick's stomach tightened. He had a sinking feeling about this development.

"I gather it's from that vessel out there," Nick responded between gritted teeth as his senses cleared. "Let's hear it."

The hidden speakers on the flight deck emitted the buzz of static, then cleared and a voice Nick knew all too well spoke. "Hey, Nick, ol' buddy. Good to see ya." It was Percy Nicely, aka Storm-crow, the murderous mercenary and wannabe warlord working for the Master. Alliance Intelligence was correct: he had survived their last encounter.

Nick swallowed hard, then cleared his throat before nodding to Gears to open the channel. "Hi, Percy, nice to hear from you, too. It's been too long."

The mercenary chuckled grimly. "I know you thought I was dead, but my clones came in very useful. You did manage to eliminate all of them while missing the *real* me." There was a short pause and it crossed Nick's mind they were about to be outflanked. Percy could be stalling before he attacked. "I suggest you better not raise your shields, including the stealth shield," said Percy, his deep voice serious. "And do not power up your weapons or my crew might get nervous and fire before I give the order." He sighed. "I would hate to have to your and your crew's deaths on my already far too crowded conscience."

Nick signaled to Gears to cut the comm. He nodded. "Options?"

"We surrender or be destroyed without firing a shot," said Siren, stating the obvious options of their predicament.

"How long until weapons are on line?" Nick asked.

"At least an hour," replied Bones, sounding very unhappy about this fact.

"Siren?"

She sighed in a surprisingly human manner. "Our shields will be up in ten minutes, but at this range they wouldn't last long. Maybe six point seven minutes at most."

"Engines, Gears?"

"I need to reset the engine control systems, which will take thirty minutes."

Nick frowned. "Could we use the materializer to transport to Percy's ship?"

"Sure," said the Kid enthusiastically. "We gonna do that? I'd really love to vaporize a few of those creeps."

"Yeah, Kid," Bones chuckled. "They'd vap you before you got a shot off. The security protocols in the materializer programming deactivates any charged energy weapons during transport. You'd get there with an empty pistol."

The Kid smirked. "Yeah, right. But we have Gears. He can rig the programming of any device known to human or alien minds."

"Will you two knock it off," Nick said gruffly. "I was thinking out loud." He rolled his eyes at the disappointed expressions of Bones and the Kid. He arched his eyebrows at them. "Sometimes I think you guys have a death wish.

"Anyone else? Any *practical* ideas?" His question ran into a wall of silence. "Never mind. Gears, open the comm again."

"You about finished over there, Nick?" Percy said over the renewed connection.

Nick sighed. "Yeah, Perc—I mean Stormcrow. Sorry." He

wanted to make a vomit sound but restrained himself. "We surrender."

"Okay," Stormcrow said his tone uncertain. "I guess I'll send over a few troopers to take you and your crew into custody."

Nick shrugged. "Sure. Why not?"

Stormcrow snorted. "Nick, I don't get it. You always have a trick or two up your sleeve. What gives with the surrender?"

"I figure if you haven't killed us already, you don't plan to. This makes me curious about your motives. Why are you following us from the Master's base of operations?"

There was a momentary pause, then Stormcrow responded. "Perhaps you and I better talk. Alone."

"What about my ship and crew?"

"Just you. I'll send your SIN transport coordinates."

"Okay then. See you in a few minutes." He signaled Gears to cut the connection.

Nick gazed at his crew, uncertain how they were going to react. Siren spoke first.

"You know this is a trap. Sir?"

Nick smirked and rose from his seat. "Yeah, I'm pretty sure Percy plans to torture me to extract information, then kill me after I've suffered horribly and after I've spilled the potatoes about the Alliance's plans."

"What's *spilled the potatoes*?" asked Bones.

Gears scowled at his large, muscular friend. "It's one of those old-timey Earth sayings Nick uses *so* annoyingly." He grunted. "I think it means he's eventually going to be forced to reveal the Alliances plans to stop the Master." He cocked one eyebrow at Nick, who nodded.

"Exactly, Bones," he said, ignoring the pilot's glare of disapproval.

"Sure, boss," said the Kid. "But why so cheerful? I wouldn't be happy to face torture."

Nick headed across the deck toward the lift, his boots echoing off the plating with each step. "I wouldn't either. But I have no plans to transport to his ship." He entered the lift car after the door slid aside to admit him. "Gears, is the System Information Network back on line?"

"Just came on line now, sir."

"SIN, have you received the coordinates?" The AI acknowledged it had. "Good, then ready the materializer."

The doors closed and Nick smiled to himself when he was alone in the lift. *This is about to get very interesting.*

10

GSS Hunter
Somewhere in uncharted space
Date unknown

NICK HELD his finger over the activation button for the materializer on the control panel. "SIN, prepare to contact them at my signal."

"Yes, Captain," replied the mechanical, emotion-free voice of the AI.

There was a momentary pause and Nick's heart began to beat faster. An anxious knot of tension formed in his belly. The rippling muscles in his arms bulged as his other hand tightened into a fist at his side. The signal had to be perfectly timed or they were all dead. Percy's sensors would detect them as soon as there was a signal connection. That was the greatest risk.

"Connect me," Nick said from between gritted teeth. He pressed the activation button at the same time as the comm connection was initiated and the object on the platform faded from view as it was broken down to its subatomic particles, which would be compressed and transmitted to the programmed destination along a tight beam of concentrated energy traveling at the speed of light. The materializer at the other end would receive the signal, capture the energy, and reassemble the object's particles in the correct order until it appeared whole once again. The process would happen in the blink of an eye.

"Rip? Mehan?" Nick froze as he waited impatiently for a reply. "SIN, external viewer." The wall opposite shimmered and became a viewer displaying Stormcrow's enormous vessel against the star field. Two smaller ships shimmered into view flanking the large ship. The ships were the ANSS *Lightning* and the *Thunder*, commanded respectively by his two handpicked captains, Rip Losp and Mehan Xsk. They had managed to make it into this space apparently undetected as he'd hoped they would.

The huge enemy vessel suddenly shuddered and started to drift as if it were out of control. The bomb they had just transported aboard her had done its job and disabled the massive warship.

"Go ahead, Captain," said Rip followed by Mehan's acknowledgement.

"Is that ship able to fire on us?" Nick asked.

"No, sir," said Mehan, her husky voice contained a hint of amusement. "Their weapons and shields are off-line. I'm detecting explosions, and some compartments have greatly elevated temperatures, which presumably means there are fires throughout the ship."

"Is their comm system still operational?"

"Yes," said Rip, his voice determined.

"Okay, both of you stand by for orders. Keep your weapons locked on, only don't fire until I determine our next steps. Though, if they somehow manage to charge a weapons battery, you are authorized to take it out immediately. Try not to destroy them in doing so. I need them alive, for the moment." The reply was a chorus of enthusiastic aye-ayes. Nick suspected they liked the idea of firing on Stormcrow's ship as the best option.

"SIN, connect me with Perc...uhhh, I mean Stormcrow."

"Nick?" came the immediate reply.

"Yeah. How's it goin'?" In the background, Nick heard a muffled explosion and the roar of an uncontrolled fire.

Stormcrow coughed, then cleared his throat. "It looks like you tricked me once again, ol' buddy." Nick rolled his eyes. He and Percy had never been friends and certainly not *old buddies*. They'd been competitors and even enemies in the years following their first meeting at the Alliance Navy Training Academy. In their time at the training academy, they locked horns in every form of hand-to-hand combat and battle simulation the navy academy offered. Sometimes Nick won, sometimes Percy won. They had about a fifty-fifty record.

"SIN, lock onto Stormcrow and transport him aboard," Nick instructed the AI.

"What about the rest of his crew?" asked the AI.

Nick's jaw tightened and his muscular, almost two-meter frame stiffened. While it seemed cruel, the rogue mercenary's crew knew they might have to pay the ultimate price for signing on to his team. Life and death were equally possible outcomes of the life mercenaries chose and of those who followed them. The least he could do was show them the mercy of a quick death.

Stormcrow shimmered into existence, kneeling on the transport pad, coughing uncontrollably due to smoke inhalation.

"Justice to *Lightning* and *Thunder*." He paused for a second or two to let the consequences of his next word sink in, then said, "Fire." His eyes shifted to the viewer showing the three ships hanging in space.

There were burst of light at the sides of the two smaller ships indicative of the launch of plasma torpedoes. The blaster cannons on the two ships lit up with rapid-fire barrages that struck the larger ship across its hull, tearing through the plating of the unshielded vessel. The large ship began to break apart and there were suddenly large explosions as the torpedoes contacted and exploded against the hull. Large jagged holes appeared, through which debris shot out into the vacuum of space. Nick's stomach muscles tightened as it occurred to him that some of the debris would be parts of alien and human bodies, blown apart by the explosions and sucked into the airless void by the rapid decompression of the ship's many compartments.

Nick's stomach soured as he thought about all the human and alien deaths he'd been responsible for until he realized it wasn't him but Stormcrow who was responsible for putting them in harm's way. He'd always seen his responsibility as captain to protect his crews, not lead them to the slaughter.

Nick pulled his blaster from the holster on his hip and strode toward the materializer platform. "On your feet, Percy," he ordered, discarding his opponent's preferred alias. The knot of angry bitterness in his gut wouldn't allow any respect for the former Alliance naval officer. Percy had gone too far off the rails and he needed to pay for his crimes against the beings of the universe.

Percy rose on shaky legs, his eyes watering, his uniform covered in soot and speckled with blood. He was unarmed, so defenseless. Secretly Nick had hoped Percy would have brandished a weapon so he could have shot him where he stood. "Let's go. You're going into the brig." He paused to steady himself. "Then you and I are going to have a talk."

Percy gazed at him and nodded in reply. His shoulders were slumped in defeat and he continued to emit deep, raspy coughs trying to clear his lungs.

"SIN, ask Siren to meet us in the brig. Tell her our prisoner is suffering from smoke inhalation."

"Yes, Captain," came the mechanical reply of the System Information Network. The artificial intelligence monitored all ship-board systems and the crew. Only Nick had the override codes for the AI. The Admiralty wasn't very happy about him having the only override codes, but Nick had insisted on this condition if he was to lead the mission.

Since he was the only captain commanding three of the most advanced warships attached to the Alliance fleet and he knew the players in the deadly game better than anyone, the navy gave in to his demands.

Of course, the navy's decision became moot when the Admiralty attempted to replace Nick with someone else; the crews essentially mutinied. Since the ships' crews were mercenaries, their response to the naval brass' interference didn't surprise Nick in the least. In fact, Bones and the Kid made it into a drinking game they called "who's the best replacement captain in the fleet." The rules mystified Nick but the hangovers each morning were evidence the game was at least a mild success.

Nick had just erected the force field in Percy's cell in the brig when Siren appeared carrying an emergency med pack. "Captain," she said, greeting Nick. "I see this is our patient." Peering into the cell where Percy sat on the bunk coughing uncontrollably, she instructed the SIN to drop the force field, then stepped into the cell, reinitializing the field behind her. She moved to stand over the enemy captain struggling to suck in fresh air between harsh coughing spells. Tears trickled down his cheeks from red-rimmed eyes.

She shifted her gaze to Nick, who stood with his arms crossed watching her from his vantage point outside the cell. "Any special instructions, sir?"

Nick grunted. "I want to say let him die, but I need him right now. He needs to talk, so allow him to breathe, and stop that infernal coughing."

Siren nodded, then set the med kit on the bed next to Percy.

She opened it and took out an injector. Retrieving a capsule the color of rubies from the depths of the kit, she shoved it into one end of the device. Siren then pressed the other end of the device into Percy's left arm near the shoulder and depressed a button on the side with her thumb. There was a sound of gas escaping.

Immediately Percy appeared to relax as his coughing eased. Siren pulled a portable breather similar to the ones used by divers and placed it between Percy's lips. The warlord sucked hungrily on the pencil-like device and color returned to his cheeks.

Finally his breathing settled to normal and he sat back on the bunk until his back was against the cell wall. "Thank you," he said to Siren.

Siren offered him a tight, humorless smile. "Don't thank me," she said, indicating Nick scowling at them from beyond the force field. Nick was secretly impressed by the faux Siren's ability to mimic the real Siren's mannerisms.

Percy looked at Nick and his shoulders slumped in defeat. "You have questions, I presume?"

Nick nodded.

11

GSS Hunter
Approaching the Hades system
4155.8.14 Galactic

THE *HUNTER* beneath him felt as if it were a wild animal eager to attack. Nick's fingers dug into the cushioned arm rests of the copilot's seat. In his mind, Nick played over and over Percy's treachery, not only to the Alliance, but how easy it had been to extract the information he needed to find the Master's war fleet. Maybe it had been too easy.

"Justice to *Thunder* and *Lightning*. Any sign of the enemy?"

"No, sir," replied Xsk, echoed by Losp. "The interference from the binary stars in the system ahead makes our long-range scans difficult and mostly unreliable," Xsk explained. "We're basically blind, sir."

Nick glanced at Gears in the pilot's seat beside him. The tech expert shrugged and nodded. This meant they were also blind. Nick snorted derisively under his breath.

These three ships had the most advanced sensors in the

known universe, yet they were useless. An entire fleet of warships could be about to appear and they would have no idea they were there until they were dead.

Percy could be leading them into a trap. Nick wouldn't put it past him. Even if they managed to find the Master's fleet in this irradiated mess of a system, their weapons' targeting scanners would prove just about as useful since they were based on the same tech as the sensors.

His guts were in a knot, signaling him to be careful. "Gears, what do you think?"

"I'd say this is a trap. Percy is a dirtbag and has been a liar as long as I've known him."

"I used my *special* tactics on him. He had a difficult time before he told me the system where his boss was assembling his invasion fleet." Nick had ordered Siren to inject a mixture of medication into Percy that would make him hallucinate and cause his nervous system to feel as if he were on fire on the inside.

The black-market med tech on a nonaligned world he had bought it from ten years ago had guaranteed the victim's pain would make anyone s*ing like a bird dog*. In truth, the alien med tech had said something less colorful, but his words reminded Nick of his grandfather's quotes from 20th century crime movies he loved. He preferred his grandfather's saying over the med tech's.

Nick had never used the medication before on anyone, and often wondered why he kept it since using banned substances made him feel dirty. But Percy had caused the death of millions, and of his best friend, so he was a special case and Nick didn't hesitate.

As far as Nick was concerned, saving the galaxy from the nightmare a megalomaniac like Asty Bonetes and his minions would inflict on the races encompassing the Alliance was the greater good. The worlds of the Alliance didn't always agree, and it wasn't perfect, but it was far preferable to being conquered by a murderous dictator who ruled by fear, threats, and a galaxy awash in innocent blood.

"Let's get closer and see if we can clean up those scans," Nick ordered. "You, too, Xsk. Losp, stay here with your stealth shields engaged and be our backstop in case we get ambushed." They needed to see if the Master's war fleet was in this system before they called in the cavalry. He expected the admiralty wasn't going to commit the majority of their forces based on Percy's intel alone. And if Percy's info was good, the Alliance Navy would need just about everything they had to stop Bonetes.

"How close?" asked Gears.

Nick's eyes shifted to the pilot, then back to the screens in front of him. "I want to know how many buttons they have on their jackets."

Gears snorted, then keyed some instructions into the flight computer and they began the slow trip to the system ahead. Nick was secretly pleased the trip would take time. It would give him time to consider a plan once they found the massive enemy fleet Percy described. The worst case involved them finding the enemy by dropping in on them suddenly, then being vaporized before they could react.

"Gears," Nick began, garnering the tech expert's attention away from his screens, "I'd like some you-and-me time. We need a plan." A slow grin spread across Gears' pale features.

12

GSS Hunter
  Hades system
  4155.8.23 Galactic

GEARS WAS RIGHT, it had taken him two days to enhance their sensor grid to penetrate the extreme radiation streaming from the two stars in this system. Nick swallowed hard and his heart rate increased when he saw the initial readings streaming across his screens.

Percy hadn't been exaggerating. Asty Bonetes' fleet was massive, far larger than the Alliance had ever encountered. Many of the ship designs were unfamiliar, indicating Bonetes had recruited his force mostly from nonaligned worlds. There was one vessel at the center of his screen, shielded by thousands of ships, that caused him to hold his breath.

It was a battlewagon so large it dwarfed all of the Alliance's first-line battlewagons combined. If the readings were correct, it was dotted with weapons of all types and it had a weapon at its center that made Nick's heart freeze with fear.

The sensor system had seen the weapon's energy signature before, in the badlands. The energy readings matched those from the robbery from the experimental laboratory on Earth in 4140.2.3 Galactic. Only the energy here was more concentrated in that massive vessel than the readings they had discovered in the badlands where they were confronted by Stormcrow's ship.

"Gears, what do you estimate is the power of that weapon?"

Gears shrugged. "It's difficult to be exact given these readings are off any known scale, but if they are capable of concentrating that energy and focusing it, it would vaporize a planet with one shot. If they deploy that weapon in any Alliance system, the best option is to surrender if survival of the population is a priority." He paused and glanced at Nick. "Even the combined forces of the Alliance Navy and all its allies are useless against that kind of power."

Nick set his jaw and narrowed his eyes. "Then we have to stop it here. The survival of the Alliance and civilization itself are dependent on us making a stand."

"Captain, the odds of us defeating a ship of that size and power are millions to one," said Siren.

"Well then, Number Two, I guess we have to die trying." Nick stood on the command deck with his arms crossed over his chest. He surveyed his loyal bridge crew, gazing upon them each in turn. Only Siren's expression seemed unfamiliar. "Blaster Squad, we have confronted every conceivable threat and survived. This time we may not, but that is the price for doing the right thing. I cannot in good conscience let Asty Bonetes conqueror the galaxy without a fight. The future is never certain, but if our time is up, then so be it." He paused to let his words sink in. "Are you with me?"

Bones grunted his usual agreement. The Kid emitted his usual *Yeah.* Gears issued an *Aye, aye, Cap'n* as he always did. But Siren's android double hesitated.

Nick arched at eyebrow at her. "Something wrong?"

"Sorry, sir, but I am carrying within me an important passenger who will eventually be reloaded into my host. It's a—concern. Sir."

Nick nodded. "I get it. But if Bonetes makes it past us into Alliance space, nothing and no one is safe. As I said, the future is unclear, but I expect the Alliance to go down fighting, and with it, most of its key worlds—including Earth, where Siren's clone is being grown. The rest of the Alliance, as Gears astutely points out, will have no choice but to surrender without firing a shot." Nick offered the android a crooked smile. "So your *passenger* will be no more unless we take every possible measure to halt Bonetes in his tracks."

"Tracks? Sir?" said the faux Siren, who was clearly confused by Nick's use of a colloquialism.

Nick chuckled. "Not important. The important thing is that we may have to deploy a weapon that has been outlawed for two millennia."

Behind him, Gears sucked in a breath. "Are you sure, Cap?" asked Bones, the shock evident on his rugged features. "I thought when we loaded that from the lunar banned weapons storage, it was being taken to an Alliance disposal facility far from Alliance space."

Nick arched an eyebrow at the weapons specialist. "Really, Bones?"

Bones cheeks flushed and he shrugged. "Well, maybe it was wishful thinking?"

Nick paused and a slow frown spread across his features. "Listen, I take sole responsibility for this bioweapon. When and if it is deployed against the enemy, I agree to bear the responsibility and I am willing to be held personally accountable for its use. None of you will be held responsible for what follows. The Alliance Chair and the Council will disavow me and condemn me as a war criminal."

"Automatic death sentence," said Gears, his voice barely above a whisper.

The Kid's features flushed and his eyes flared with anger. "Really? The Captain saves their asses and they execute him? That isn't right." He slammed his fist on the arm of his chair. "The Alliance has killed millions in pursuit of Bonetes and his followers. Whole planets have been decimated and no one is held accountable for those deaths."

Nick shook his head. "This is different. This weapon is biological, and while it will kill Bonetes and his followers with absolute certainty, if it gets beyond this system it will potentially kill trillions, far more than Bonetes might."

He paused to let his words sink in, then added. "This virus is the most deadly ever devised and should have been destroyed a millennia ago. The Alliance kept it stored in absolute secrecy in the most heavily guarded and secure facility in the galaxy in an airless, sterile containment field. Knowledge of this weapon is beyond top secret. I was briefed by the head of Alliance Security about the weapon, its history, methods of deployment, the dangers, and its effects on victims."

He stood and walked across the cabin, debating with himself how much more to tell his loyal squad. "The virus is called Prometheus and it mutates when attacked by any antivirus known to Alliance science. On contact with an oxygen-rich environment, the pathogen can kill in about four seconds. Each victim—even in death—becomes a host as the virus spreads through a population faster than anyone can react. In truth, there is nowhere to run and nowhere to hide from this monster.

"And if anyone's thinking the virus can't affect nonhuman races, think otherwise. The mutative properties of this virus mean it can adapt to the biology of any lifeform." He paused to survey the horrified faces of his friends. "I can't tell you anything more. In fact I may have told you more than I should have."

"How do we deliver this virus?" Bones asked, his muscular arms crossed over his chest.

Nick's eyes became hard, dark points. "I'm taking it aboard that enemy ship out there and releasing it into their environment."

13

GSS Hunter
 Hades system
 4155.8.24 Galactic

IT HAD TAKEN Bones a day to navigate them to within transport distance of the massive battlewagon that filled the forward view screen of the *Hunter*. It looked more like a moon or large asteroid than a starship. Only starships weren't usually bristling with the weapons package this ship displayed. Nick had never seen such firepower on one vessel. If the ship launched everything at an Alliance naval target, it would be shredded into confetti before the crew could respond. Shielding might slow the barrage down, but not enough to make any appreciable difference at an attack of this magnitude.

So far there hadn't been any indication that the enemy had penetrated their stealth shields. Once the materializer was activated, this would change. Nick instructed Gears to make an abrupt course change and flee the system as quickly as possible. As a last resort, Gears would engage the FTL drive in-system in order to escape. The displacement wave would cause the binary stars to go nova, but the system was uninhabited so no innocents would be vaporized. Only the Master's people would be wiped out, and that didn't bother anyone since they were far from innocent.

Of course, the total destruction of a binary star system would disrupt thousands of inhabited systems across the quadrant for millions of light years in every direction. The consequences of their actions would be difficult to predict, and it made Nick sick to think of the unnecessary deaths that were more than likely to occur by the displacement of these stars. Engaging the FTL drive in the system had to be the last resort. Gears and Nick were of one mind when it came to sparing innocent lives.

Those additional deaths were laid at the Master's feet. Nick's hands formed fists, and a knot of anger began in his belly. Bonetes would pay for his crimes.

The *Lightning* was ordered to stay hidden behind one of the outer planet's rocky moons within the system with their stealth shields engaged, in reserve in case the *Hunter* was detected and destroyed. In that event, their orders were to make a suicide run and try to pierce the shielding of the enemy command ship. Once inside their shields, the *Lightning* would breach their own plasma and nuclear fuel tanks, causing a massive explosion to hopefully destroy the enemy vessel.

The *Thunder* would then engage their FTL drive as they entered the system, thereby destroying the remainder of the enemy fleet. Blaster Squad would be dead, but if everything went right, so would the Master and his minions.

"We almost ready, Gears?" Nick asked, his voice calm, resigned to his fate.

"Yes, Captain."

"Okay, I'll be in the materializer bay in fifteen." Nick turned slightly in his seat and looked at Bones. The weapons specialist's eyes were hard points of coal. "The weapon ready?" Bones nodded. "Good. Meet me in the materializer bay with the containment device and we'll get this show on the road."

"What show?" asked Siren.

The Kid laughed grimly. "He means the mission, Siren."

She shook her head. "A mission is *not* a show."

"No, it isn't, Number Two, you are very definitely right about that," said Nick, followed by a derisive grunt. He rose from his seat and walked across the flight deck, his boot steps echoing off the quiet wall of tension that had fallen over the crew.

Before entering the lift to take him to the materializer bay, Nick faced his crew and said, "We need to do our jobs. It's what we do. And we do it very well."

He turned back to the lift doors, then stepped inside when the doors opened. He kept his back to his friends until the doors closed. Turning around, he released the deep breath he'd been holding. This could well be the last time he would see them and he didn't want them to see the fear in his eyes.

The lift doors opened onto the materializer bay and he stepped out. The doors whooshed shut behind him. He had time to don a breather suit and a personal stealth shield before Bones arrived with the weapon. He went to the storage closet and selected a breather suit and a portable shield generator.

The lift doors opened and Bones entered the bay carrying a sealed plasti-steel tube in his left, gloved hand. The purplish liquid in the tube glowed, giving off heat as the virus behind the glass worked hard to get out of the containment field in the tube. The virus was a living organism, and like any organic lifeform, desired its freedom.

Bones waited while Nick finished dressing. "Nothing more to say?" Nick asked as he set his breather suit helmet on the front edge of the waist-high materializer control console.

"You've made your decision, Captain." Bones features were calm, but Nick could see the distress in his eyes. He had been opposed to bringing this deadly bioweapon aboard from the beginning. At the time he had sensed something too terrible to contemplate was going to happen with it. As it turned out, Bones was right.

Nick walked to the weapons locker and found the rifle he would use to deliver the weapon. It was designed to hold the glass tube. One end of the tube would be fitted with a rubber tip with a razor sharp needle sticking from the tip. Once he pressed the firing stud, a gas cartridge would eject the tube at high speed at a target and the needle would pierce the target, releasing the virus. Unless Nick's suit was ripped or the seal broken in some way, he would be transported back to the *Hunter* after he deployed the weapon. They would be awaiting his signal to bring him back aboard. If he failed to signal them within an hour from now, they were to execute plan B, and plan C if plan B failed.

Once released into the environment, the virus would destroy all organic lifeforms aboard the enemy vessel. It would become a plague ship. Nick held faint hope the enemy would not check the sensor readings too closely and transport aboard to look for survivors and themselves be quickly overcome as well. It was probably asking too much that they might even transport back to their ships and infect those crews too, but Nick could dream.

Nick affixed the rubber tip with the needle sticking from the rubber, loaded the glass tube carefully into the breach, then secured it by closing the breach door. He breathed a sigh of relief that the deadly virus was now secure and ready to be used. His stomach was churning at the thought about the power of life and death now in his hands.

He swallowed to steady his nerves, then placed the rifle in the specially designed sling Gears had made for him than slung the rifle across his back. All he had to do was reach over his left shoulder, grab the gun, aim, and fire.

After placing the helmet over his head, he locked it in place.

The heads-up display in the helmet's faceplate showed the atmosphere in the suit was normal. He stepped onto the materializer platform, and after nodding to Bones, who had moved to operate the control panel, he tapped the controls of the personal shield generator affixed to his arm to set the stealth shield.

He held his breath when he felt the familiar tingling as the materializer began to separate his atoms for transport. The next thing he saw was an empty corridor shrouded in semi-darkness. The faceplate adjusted for the low light environment. He saw doors running away from him along a curved wall until they disappeared around the curve. The opposite wall was devoid of doors, access panels, or any other adornment; it was painted a dull gray color.

Reluctant to pull the virus rifle, Nick instead pulled his blaster from the holster on his hip and began to slowly walk toward the curve in the corridor. He kept the blaster in front of him ready for any sudden movements from the doors as he moved past each one. He occasionally looked behind him in case someone had exited a door after he passed it. So far he was alone. His heart rate increased with each passing minute as adrenaline surged into his blood stream.

I should have insisted Bones transport me to the command bridge. Not that it mattered who he shot with the virus, but Bonetes might have been on the bridge. After he told him he'd been injected with a terminal virus, Nick would have enjoyed the shock on the would-be emperor's face when he realized he was about to die. Then, of course, Nick would also be dead after Bonetes' bodyguards killed him. But it would have been a win-win scenario as far as he was concerned. But Bones and Gears convinced him his death was unnecessary to complete the mission. Reluctantly he concluded his old friends were right.

With startling swiftness, four heavily armed, battle armor-wearing troopers appeared suddenly, surrounding him. Two troopers restrained his arms while the other two disarmed him, including relieving him of the modified rifle still in its specially designed sleeve. Nick's stealth shield disappeared and he became visible.

"Be careful with that rifle." Nick's tone was low and menacing. He smiled to himself when he saw the arrogant expression on the trooper's face and in his eyes. He didn't respond, just gave one of the other troopers a slight nod of his head. Something was very wrong with all this. It was as if they'd been expecting him and somehow knew about the virus rifle.

One of the troopers grabbed his arms and pulled them behind his back, placed force binders around his wrists, and activated them. Nick winced due to the pain when the trooper tightened them, then two sets of strong hands grabbed him by his arms and he was guided down the corridor.

This will not end well, Nick concluded.

14

Enemy Command Ship
  Hades system
  4155.8.24 Galactic

Two of the troopers stayed behind while the other two shoved Nick forcefully aboard a lift car. The doors closed. "Deck one," said the trooper, gripping his left arm a little too tightly in Nick's opinion. *That's going to leave one hell of a bruise.*

The car began to move and soon the doors opened on an unbelievable scene. Nick was shoved into the vast chamber before him, his jaw hanging open in awe. The floor was black marble and there were full-sized statues of Roman and Greek gods, and life-like figures of what Nick assumed were Roman emperors lining the floor to ceiling tapestry-covered walls. There were also statues Nick didn't recognize, though some might have been from human history. A statue of a short white Earthman, wearing calf-high black leather boots and cradling a strange looking hat in the crook of one arm, had one hand buried inside his dark blue vest.

Another statue depicted another Earthman, a small, dark

mustache over his upper lip, dressed in a quasi-military uniform, a blood-red armband on the left arm displaying a black symbol reminiscent of a twisted cross against a white background. The insanity evident in the figures' glass eyes made Nick involuntarily shiver.

Other statues lining the walls of the vast space were of various Alliance despots from across the history of known space. While Nick didn't recognize every one of them, the ones he did recognize each had committed unimaginable atrocities against their planet's populations in pursuit of wealth and/or power.

It was a museum to madness and mass murder, something Nick had fought against as the leader of Blaster Squad. *I really need to reassess my plan.* The thought of wiping out an enemy with a weapon of mass destruction such as a biological weapon made him feel suddenly sick to his stomach. *Mass murderer isn't who I am.*

Nick realized it was the ranks of these murderous humans and aliens Bonetes apparently craved to join. Only he planned to win what they had lost: absolute power. Power fueled by fear, death, and blood.

The troopers walked Nick across the open space toward a raised podium with three steps to a dais where an unoccupied, ornate golden throne rested, sparkling under the subdued lightning. Once they released his arms, Nick scanned the chamber. He looked to one of the troopers standing to his left, his hands folded waist high in front of him. "Where's Bonetes?" The Trooper stared at him with a sneer on his face. It was clear he wasn't saying anything. The force binders were beginning to itch.

"Well then, why am I still alive? I assume Bonetes knows I've been captured."

"Yes, of course," said a voice reminiscent of crunching gravel.

From the left side of the throne dais, a tall human male appeared from the shadows. He was dressed in gleaming black battle armor trimmed with gold strips of leather along the sleeves and down the outside of both trouser legs. A tattoo of a hawk's head adorned the left side of his chiseled olive-skinned features and his oil-black hair was slicked back ending with a small ponytail at the back of his square head. He appeared fit and muscular, filling out the body armor with his sinewy frame.

Two heavily armed guards appeared, following him from the shadows. One was human, at least in outward appearance, the other was a massive four-armed Lobsan. They each wore body armor unlike any Nick had seen before, decorated with ornate carvings of vines and fierce animals such as lions and tigers, and they each had a short sword as part of the weapons belt surrounding their thick waists.

"Asty Bonetes, I presume," said Nick.

The man smirked, though there was no humor in the hard, coal-black eyes. He went up the three steps of the dais and sat in the throne before responding. "The name is Emperor Astrid the First."

Nick looked Bonetes in the eyes and realized the mind behind those eyes was as mad as a March rabbit as his grandfather used to say. He could antagonize this self-proclaimed emperor or play along with his delusions until he had an opening to retrieve the virus. Uncertainty gripped Nick about what his next steps would be from here on. The original plan wasn't as easy as he had thought it would be.

He decided antagonizing Bonetes might only trigger a quick end to Nick's mission and that wouldn't serve anyone's interests. He sighed inwardly. *Playing along it is.*

Nick nodded. "Of course, Emperor. I didn't know you'd already assumed the throne. My apologies."

One side of Bonetes' mouth curled upward and his eyes flared. The bastard was enjoying this more than Nick intended. His fingers curled into fists and his heart rate increased. "What do you want with me, Emperor?"

Bonetes sat forward in the throne. The ironic smile evaporated and his eyes glared at Nick. "I need to know the Alliance fleet's deployment strategy. How many ships, their sizes and armaments, and what star systems they will be in and when."

Nick arched an eyebrow at Bonetes. "And why would I give you any of that information?"

Bonetes snorted. He nodded his head at the center of the room behind Nick.

Looking around, Nick witnessed a three-dimensional image shimmer into existence. He recognized it as a visual representation of a map of the star system. On the map were icons indicating what Nick assumed were starships with thousands of green icons representing the enemy fleet, Bonetes' flagship at the center of a wheel-shaped ring of ships. There were three purple icons Nick was certain were the positions of Blaster Squad's ships. One was orbiting a moon around a gas giant in the outer system. One was at the edge of the system, and one was near Bonetes' flagship.

Nick swallowed hard as bile rose to the back of his throat. Someone on his team was a traitor.

15

Enemy Command Ship
   Hades system
   4155.8.24 Galactic

"IF I TELL you what you need to know, will you guarantee my squad's safety? I don't care what happens to me." Nick stared into the dark, emotionless eyes of the would-be emperor seeking any sign of humanity, but instead saw only a reflection of the black soul of a brutal psychopath bent on destruction. A shiver of fear traveled the length of Nick's spine, but he was determined not let it show to this monster.

"I guarantee nothing more than a short and painless death for you and your crews. Nothing will stand in the way our conquest of the Alliance." Bonetes arched an eyebrow at Nick, suggesting failure to comply would result in the opposite of short and painless. "Blaster Squad has disrupted my plans for years. I need you and your crew out of my way. Permanently." Bonetes shrugged. "How you meet your death is your decision."

A sense of dread for the lives of his friends threatened to overwhelm Nick. He had looked away while Bonetes spoke but now shifted his gaze back to psychopath. "Okay," he said in a low voice.

Bonetes chuckled. "You think I'm foolish enough to believe you so easily?" He raised one hand palm up to his Lobsan guard, who nodded, then turned and disappeared into the shadows.

Within moments of the guard's disappearance, the scene on the three-dimensional visual display changed as six green icons began converging on the moon in a classic flanking maneuver. The purple icon must be the *Lightning*. Nick hoped Gears had resolved their sensor capability issues as he had on the *Hunter*. Without sensors, they would be unable to detect the incoming attack. They wouldn't know their stealth shield was useless. He swallowed hard and his mouth became dry.

"How did you defeat our stealth shields?" Nick asked Bonetes.

Bonetes snorted derisively. "Really? That's your biggest concern?" he pointed toward the quickly converging icons.

"What can I tell you to make you call off the attack?" said Nick unable to keep the desperation from his voice.

Bonetes shook his head. "Nothing. I need to make a point and the destruction of one of your ships will make my point." A crooked grin crossed his lips. "At least their deaths will be short and sweet." His eyebrows gathered above his dark eyes to transform to a glare. "I won't be so generous again."

Nick turned his attention to the display, desperate for any sign the *Lightning*'s crew knew they had to escape. Suddenly a second purple icon appeared next to the first one. It was there no more than a minute or two, then disappeared once again. Nick blinked, uncertain if he had seen what he thought he saw.

"Find them!" shouted Bonetes, now standing on the throne dais, his features twisted by rage. His eyes flitted briefly to Nick. "Put him in the cells. I'll deal with him later."

Nick smiled to himself as he was led away toward the lifts. Gears had come through once again. While being spared for the moment was a good thing, the identity of the traitor weighed heavily on his mind.

16

Enemy Command Ship
Hades system
Unknown Galactic

NICK HAD BEEN WRACKING his brain for the entire time he'd been sitting on the bunk in this cell, trying to think of times he suspected one of his friends might be working for Bonetes or one of his associates. The energy field preventing him from leaving the cell hummed in the quiet. He had no sense of time's passage nor any sense of movement in the vessel around him. The cell's smooth, bare, plasti-steel walls gave him no clues.

No one had visited him, and no guards appeared with offers of a last meal for the condemned man. He wondered why Bonetes kept him alive now that it appeared Blaster Squad had once again escaped his trap. *All except me,* he thought, looking round at his meager surroundings. "Good thing they provided a waste disposal unit," he murmured glumly.

He wondered for the umpteenth time how he would get out of

here, and he wondered how the squad was faring after their escape.

Suddenly the outer door to the cells slid open and a guard he hadn't seen before entered. He seemed familiar. The ambling walk and the square jaw showing under the rim of the blast shield covering the majority of the face coupled with the broad shoulders and muscular arms could only mean one person. The door swooshed closed behind the guard, who paused, then lifted the blast shield to reveal Bones' smiling features looking back at Nick.

"How?" Nick sputtered.

"Ya know, Cap'n, Gears always has a few tricks up his greasy sleeves."

Nick's grin soon faded and his heart threatened to skip a beat. "Where are the guards?"

"Never mind that right now." Bones slapped down the visor. "We have to get out of here." He approached the control panel for the cells, recessed into the wall opposite the force field separating them. He appeared to study the panel for several seconds, then pulled his blaster from his holster and shot the controls, which erupted in a shower of sparks and billowing smoke. The force field flickered once, then disappeared.

"What do ya know?" Bones murmured.

Nick stepped out of the cell trying, but failing, to hide his amusement. Bones loved shooting first and asking questions the other day, or something like that. Technology was never his strong suit except when it came to all classes of energy weapons.

The door to the corridor slid open revealing it was empty. "Follow me," said Bones in a low voice, his blaster held at the ready.

They stepped into the corridor with Nick right behind his muscular friend. "Where we goin'?" Nick whispered.

"We have to make it to an unshielded section of the ship so the SIN can transport us out," came the reply.

Nick had never heard of partially penetrating a ship's shielding. How was this possible? He sighed to himself.

"No more questions, Cap'n."

With Gears, the impossible was usually possible. *I'm gonna have to add a bonus to his next pay.* Of course, they hadn't been paid for the past three years, but at least the thought was a good one.

They hurried down the empty corridor and Nick wondered why they hadn't seen anyone yet. Was the ship on nighttime operations? Bones said no more questions. It was driving him crazy. Nick had *so* many questions and he'd just been broken out of the cells moments before.

They moved quickly, not pausing to check for threats as they rounded each bend in the corridor. Bones seemed unconcerned they might run into armed guards or random crewmembers. None of this made much sense. It was almost as if Bones had thrown the handbook out the airlock.

Nick wished now he had created a handbook for Blaster Squad. *Writing a handbook is now at the top of my to do list as soon as this mission is over.*

Bones signaled with a raised fist they were to hold in front of a door. There was no indication what was behind the door; in fact, it looked much like any other gray door they'd passed on the way here. The door slid open to reveal a cadre of armed troopers and a grinning Bonetes, his muscular arms crossed over his wide chest.

"Come in, Justice," Bonetes said, his voice heavy with sarcasm. Bones stepped aside to let Nick enter ahead of him. Nick glared at the would-be emperor. Bonetes grinned and his dark eyes sparkled with amusement. "I'm always one step ahead of you, Nick. This time your luck has run out."

"We weren't *lucky*, we were good," Nick said in a low growl.

Bonetes chuckled and arched an eyebrow at Nick. "You know, Nick, you could be right about that, which is why I fixed the game between us. I see you've met my deep cover agent." He nodded toward Bones, who still had the faceplate down covering most of his face.

"What did he offer you, Bones? Money? Power? What, damn you!" Nick's guts boiled in anger. Bones was one of his oldest friends. He'd been at his side going back to their days at the Alliance Naval Academy.

"My own planet," Bones said in low menacing voice.

Nick snorted derisively. "You know I can't compete with *that*," he said sarcastically, "but what about honor, integrity, fighting the good fight to save innocent lives?"

Bones flipped up his faceplate, revealing an angry glare directed at Nick. "That pathetically weak stuff doesn't put food on my table. You've always treated me as furniture with a gun."

Nick froze. He was right...in a way. But this still didn't add up to Bones turning on him to join this megalomaniac's twisted dreams. "I'm sorry, Bones, I had no idea..."

A sardonic grin broke over Bones dusky features. "That's Centurion Bones." His dark eyes flicked to Bonetes, then back to Nick. "But soon I'll be called the Imperial Governor of Mars." He beamed with pride. "Then they'll respect me on Mars."

Nick swallowed his next words. Bones was a hero to the people of Mars. His heroics in saving countless civilizations since joining Blaster Squad was well known and his exploits were celebrated across the planet. Numerous accounts were written about his adventures and every city had a plaque honoring his visits.

Suddenly Nick stiffened as the familiar tingle of a materializer beam enveloped him. The room around him began to fade. The last sounds he heard before disappearing were angry shouts by Bonetes, urging his troopers to shoot them.

His next realization of his surroundings was a materializer bay aboard one of his Blaster Squad ships and a grinning Gears standing behind the control panel.

"Hey, Captain. Nice to have you back among us," the tech specialist said. "SIN, get us out of here."

Nick suddenly realized Bones was standing next to him. "Gears, confinement beam on Bones now!"

Bones and Gears began laughing. "No, sir, you don't understand..." choked out Gears.

"Gears. He turned me over to Bonetes. He wants to be the imperial governor of Mars."

Bones placed a hand on Nick's shoulder. "Com'on, Cap'n. Do I look like the administrator type or a politician? Really?" He chuckled. "Bonetes believed I turned on you when I supplied him false information about our ship movements." Stepping off the materializer platform, Bones joined Gears behind the control console.

Turning to face Nick, he continued. "I've been a double agent for Alliance Intelligence for the past two years. They suspected Bonetes was behind the Master's plans and they needed someone on the inside of his organization." He shrugged. "Since I'm a weapons expert, they felt this would attract Bonetes' ambitions and feed his enormous ego." He slapped Gears on the back, startling the smaller man, who turned and scowled at his large friend. "It wasn't really that hard. The guy's kind of easy to impress."

"Excuse me," said a familiar voice over the comm. "A dozen enemy ships are closing on our position. They will be in firing range in twenty point seven-two minutes." Siren's doppelganger must be on the bridge with the Kid. *I'm on the* Hunter. Nick smiled to himself. *Good.*

There remained a serious problem. If Bonetes remained in control of the bio virus, he could decimate whole worlds, then take over without firing a shot. "SIN, location of the bio weapon?"

The AI replied without hesitation. "It resides in the sterile security vault aboard the *Hunter*, sir."

Nick shifted his gaze between Gears and Bones, who avoided

him, their eyes locked on the console. "I never had the bio weapon with me, did I?"

Bones cleared his throat. "Uh, no, sir..." he paused, "we needed a distraction so the Kid could plant some bombs..."

Nick stepped off the materializer platform. "You mean I was a decoy?"

Gears cleared his throat this time. "Sir...Nick...we couldn't let you sacrifice yourself so we came up with another—a better—plan."

Nick grunted. "They could have killed me the moment I transported aboard."

Bones shook his head. "Not if I told them you were coming. Sir."

Nick looked aghast at his friend. "You told them? Why?"

"So you'd be captured rather than killed on sight. Bonetes told me your capture was a very large feather in his cap. We decided to rescue you after we pulled out the *Lightning*'s crew. Knowing how nuts the guy is when crossed, there was a high probability Bonetes would have had you executed once he caught up with us."

"Twelve minutes until they achieve firing range," Siren said over the comm.

Nick eyed Bones with one eyebrow cocked. "You mean as in twelve minutes from now?" He let out a breath. "Where did the Kid plant the bombs?" He scanned his friends' sheepish faces.

Gears shrugged and Bones' features flushed red. "He planted them near the plasma drive fuel tank on their command ship," Gears said before Bones could respond. "By the way, they call that ship the *Emperor's Blood*. Ironic, isn't it?" He offered Nick a weak grin.

"Because he's going to be killed when the bombs go off and I assume he's going to bleed?" Nick said quietly. Gears nodded. Involuntarily, Nick rolled his eyes.

"We have one problem, Cap'n," said Bones.

"And what might that be?"

"They captured the Kid after he planted the bombs."

Nick sighed. "So your perfect plan has gone sideways. Are the bombs still ready to go?" Bones nodded grimly. Nick's heart almost skipped a beat as a thought occurred to him "Is the Kid alive?" Bones looked away. Gears shrugged. *They don't know where the Kid is or if he's still alive. Great. Now I've got a bigger mess to clean up.*

"Guys, next time you have your own plan, maybe you better check with me first. Okay?" They nodded in unison.

"We're going to talk more about this, but for now we've got a squad member to rescue and a galaxy to save." He grinned at them. "Let's get to the bridge. We've got work to do."

17

GSS Hunter
Hades system
4155.8.25 Galactic

"SIN, locate the Kid on the command ship," Nick said as soon as he was seated in the copilot's station, his eyes flitting across the readings on the incoming ships. They were trying to encircle the *Hunter* as if creating a net in space.

"That vessel is one hundred million kilometers from our current position," explained the AI.

"Just do it," Nick said with a snort of frustration. He turned slightly in his seat. "Gears, you created something that would mirror our position to an enemy's sensors, correct?"

Gears looked at Nick, his brow wrinkled. "Yes, sir, I did," his voice betraying his surprise.

"That's how you made them think the *Lightning* was in orbit around that moon when you suddenly appeared to rescue them." The tech genius grinned. "Of course, neither the *Hunter* nor the *Lightning* were anywhere near that location. Both ships were sensor echoes." He chuckled grimly. "Bonetes must have been furious when he realized he'd been fooled."

Gears shrugged. "Apoplectic is probably a better word choice in his case." A look of disgust came over his face. "I've never heard so much foul language used over a comm, ever." He looked thoughtful for a second, then added, "What's an elephant's sphincter extrusion?"

"I'll explain later," said Nick with a chuckle. "Right now I need you to make us disappear from those attacking vessels' sensors in..." he turned back look at Siren. "How long?"

"They will be in firing range in eight point six minutes," she said from her post at sensor control.

"The Kid has broken out of the brig aboard the enemy ship," reported the SIN.

"Good," said Nick, his heart pounding with excitement. His plan might actually work. "Can we reach him over the long-range comm?"

"Yes, sir, but the signal will be detected."

Nick turned to Gears. "Eight minutes." Gears nodded and began keying instructions into the screen to his right of the three in front of him.

"SIN, prepare to transport the Kid aboard in seven minutes. Exactly," he emphasized. "Bones. Weapons?" Nick said.

"Fully charged and ready on your command, Cap'n," replied the weapons expert.

Nick smiled to himself. This was about to get very interesting and dangerous. "Okay, everyone, this is going to be a rough ride."

"Two point two minutes," reported Siren.

Nick tapped the comm icon on his screen. "Kid, this is the Captain. Prepare for transport in one minute." He cut the connection.

His body tensed and time seemed to slow down. "Gears, set course to take us back to the enemy command ship—"

"You mean the *Emperor's Blood*?" Gears said, being annoyingly precise as usual.

"Yes. Just plot the course and be ready to make the correction when you engage the ghost ship doodad."

"The Kid is aboard the *Hunter*, sir," said the SIN.

Gears gasped. "Captain, I must protest—"

"Thirty seconds," said Siren, cutting off all other conversation.

Gears dropped into silence, preparing to engage the device to disguise the course change they were about to make.

"Now," said Siren.

Gears tapped the screen to his left and they felt an increase in g-force as the antigravity system strained to compensate for the abrupt course change. Nick thought he could detect a slight odor of burned circuits.

"The enemy ships are following the false sensor image, sir," reported Siren. "They are firing a plethora of plasma and blaster cannons at the image coordinates."

"Simulating a massive explosion of plasma and nuclear fuel tanks should convince them to leave the area." Gears wiggled his eyebrows at Nick. "And convince them we're dead."

Nick grinned. "That's some new toy you've come up with, Gears. I'm impressed." Gears cringed slightly at the toy word, but otherwise appeared pleased for the praise.

"So, what's the plan?" asked Bones, interrupting the Gears-is-great moment.

Nick smiled to himself. Bones had always been slightly envious of Gears' ability to fix or create anything technical to get them out of their latest scrape. Bones' preferred approach often involved shooting first and asking questions after the smoke cleared.

A grinning, soot-covered Kid appeared from the lift and sprinted to his seat on the bridge. Nick nodded at the younger man.

"The Kid will trigger the bomb to rupture the nuclear fuel tank first to cause a panic aboard the *Emperor's Blood*, and as a signal to Bonetes he has failed once again. Then shortly after we'll rupture the plasma tank, which will likely result in the destruction of the ship. The resulting explosion of such a large amount of volatile plasma fuel should take out a lot of the enemy ships before they can escape."

Nick's mouth dried and his heart beat faster as he thought of the lives they were about to end. But the people and aliens who followed Bonetes must have known they might end their lives in violent ways. The madman was leading them off a cliff, but it still created some doubt in Nick's mind if he was doing the right thing.

Then, of course, there was the loss of life in the Alliance during a war with the enemy fleet he had to consider as the priority. The destruction of Bonetes' fleet and their crews was, on balance, the greater good. Armed with this realization, it made those deaths more palatable.

Pushing aside his doubts, Nick focused instead on the mission at hand. "SIN, how long until we reach the enemy fleet?"

"At present velocity we will be at the designated coordinates in thirty-three minutes, approximately," replied the AI. Nick thought he could hear the hesitation in the AI's response. SIN really hated being inexact, but Nick told the AI to use approximations when it could, leaving it up to the SIN to determine the correct occasions to be inexact. Like any learning machine, the AI was getting good at picking its moments.

"Kid, how close do we have to be to activate the bombs?"

"Any distance really, sir," replied the Kid. "There isn't any reason to be closer than half a light year given we can send the signal using the FTL comm signal booster."

Nick considered this new information carefully. He had never heard of an FTL comm signal booster, no doubt another of Gears' inventions. Regardless, he wanted to be within short sensor range to record the destruction in detail. They had to be able to assure the Alliance Navy they'd destroyed Bonetes' command ship and a large portion of his fleet, so the navy knew as exactly as possible what they were up against.

"Okay, let's come within a half million kilometers before we set off the first bomb." He glanced at Gears. "I gather your new stealth shield will keep us undetected?" The tech genius nodded, his expression confident. "Are you able to use your doodad to generate a sensor image showing the *Hunter* is fifty thousand kilometers off the *Emperor's Blood*'s port bow?"

"From half million kilometers, sir?" asked Gears, his brow wrinkled.

Nick arched one eyebrow at the tech genius.

"Yes, sir, easy as strudel." Gears grinned.

Nick smirked. The saying was actually easy as cake, meaning the task was simple, but this wasn't the time to correct his old friend. He'd explain it to him later.

"Siren, is there a moon or large asteroid within half a million kilometers of the command ship where we can hide just in case?"

"Yes, sir. The enemy fleet is orbiting a massive gas giant with over forty moons in its orbit. One of those moons should suit us perfectly."

"Good. Pick one orbiting at about the right distance from the gas giant and send the coordinates to Gears. Everyone else be prepared in case they somehow penetrate our shields." Gears scowled at him. Nick shrugged. When the tech genius said something worked, it worked perfectly every time. Regardless, Nick wasn't about to take any chances given what had happened before.

They were soon in position and both Siren and the SIN were scanning the enemy fleet with sensors attempting to cover as many of the over three thousand vessels in orbit around the gas giant as possible. "Kid, you ready to set off the first explosion?"

"Yes, Captain," the Kid said, his voice tight due to the import of the moment.

"That's odd..." said Siren, her voice trailing off. "These readings don't make sense."

"What, Siren?"

"Well, sir, the enemy ships are mostly derelicts. They are far too ancient to be much good up against a Mark Nine Alliance Navy cargo ship, never mind a heavy cruiser or even a two-person picket ship," she explained.

Nick paused to consider this new information. "Why didn't we pick this up earlier?"

"We were concentrating our sensors on the command ship," said Gears. "What does this mean?"

"It's another damned trap," Bones spit out bitterly.

Nick's lips pursed. Initially he thought that as well. Too many aspects of the past few missions had gone awry for his liking, but this time didn't feel like the others. "No, I don't think so. Gears, use that FTL comm booster to hail the nearest Alliance Naval ship."

"Yes, sir." The tech genius concentrated on his middle screen. A satisfied look came over his face. "I have Admiral Jameson."

"Jack. Good to hear your voice." Jack Jameson had been in his academy graduating class. They'd been self-defense training and drinking buddies in those days. The drinking was to lessen the pain of the bruises and cuts they'd each suffered from the self-defense training.

"Hey, is that Nick Justice?" said a gruff man's voice.

"Sure is, ol' buddy." Nick paused for effect. It was time for serious business. "Jack, what's the situation with the fleet?"

"Is this line secure?"

Nick eyes flitted to Gears, who nodded. "Go ahead, Jack."

Jack sucked in a breath, then said, "We've been ordered to the Earth system. Scouts reported in approximately three days ago that an enemy fleet composed of four battlewagons, larger than anything we have ever seen, accompanied by thousands of smaller cruisers and destroyers will enter the system. Alliance Command

Headquarters have received a transmission from someone calling himself Emperor Astrid the First, demanding the Alliance unconditionally surrender to him."

Nick smirked to himself. Bonetes must have left the command ship as soon as Nick was locked in the brig. "That so-called emperor, Jack, is Asty Bonetes aka the Master, who has been causing havoc across the galaxy these past few years." Nick's forehead wrinkled in thought.

"Listen, Jack, I know the Council will never surrender to this madman, nor do I think we need to. I have a plan in mind. I'll rendezvous with the fleet at coordinates Gears will send you."

"Okay, Nick, I hope you know what you're doing."

"Jack, if we fail the Alliance dies forever, so we have limited choices ahead of us. See you soon." Nick signaled for Gears to cut the connection.

He sat silently in his chair, thinking about their next move. "Kid, set off those bombs, and Gears, set course for a spot half a light year from Earth's system. Engage the FTL drive when ready."

"Sir?" said Gears, his face drained of color.

Nick glanced at the pilot and sighed. "Just do it. And signal to *Thunder* they are to follow our lead."

18

GSS Hunter
   One hundred million kilometers from the Sol System
   4155.8.27 Galactic

"Is it as bad as Jack Jameson told us?" asked Nick. He had just swallowed the last of his avocado and peanut protein bar when his tri-screens lit up with icons showing thousands of vessels on course for Earth.

When the *Hunter* and the *Thunder* had rendezvoused with the Alliance fleet earlier that day, Siren had programmed their sensors to report only non-Alliance ships. He didn't need polluted readings until they knew what they were about to face.

The Alliance had assembled the largest fleet ever deployed, with forty-eighty battlewagons, three hundred heavy cruisers, two thousand destroyer class vessels, and one thousand picket ships, which Nick hoped, but doubted, would be enough to destroy the enemy fleet. Or even slow them down much given the energy weapon they'd discovered on the command ship in the badlands. *Maybe they didn't all carry those high-energy weapons...*

"Yes, sir," replied Siren. "In fact, they have acquired at least two more of those large battlewagons for a total of six that size, and with the armaments of the command ship we destroyed in the Hades system."

"SIN, calculate the odds the Alliance fleet will repel those ships using conventional tactics before they reach Earth."

"Less than five percent, approximately," replied the AI.

Nick's lips formed a grim line. The AI had started making nearly perfect estimates. *Too bad*, he thought. "Kid, open the inter-ship comm, but only to the *Thunder*. I don't want anyone else listening in, not even the navy."

"Go ahead, sir."

"Yes, sir?" It was Mehan Xsk, Captain of the *Thunder*.

"Are you and Rip ready?" The *Thunder* had rescued the *Lightning*'s captain and crew before the enemy patrol ships destroyed it in the Hades system.

"Yes, sir. Gears helped us update our stealth shields programming, and he provided the specs for the sensor ghost technology. Rip's and my chief engineers were able to make the changes and upgrade the sensors after we left the Hades system in plenty of time for the mission."

"Okay, good." Nick shifted his gaze to Gears in the pilot's seat and nodded. "Gears, to *Thunder*. We will engage the stealth shields on my mark." He tapped an icon in the middle of his three screens. "Mark."

Nick thought they might disappear, then smiled to himself when they obviously didn't. "Set course for the enemy fleet and engage at point nine-nine FTL."

"SIN, how long until intercept?"

"Approximately Thirty two minutes."

"Okay, everyone, let's get our weapons systems ready. SIN, integrate navigation with weapons." He looked to Gears. "Give the attack order on my signal, not before. Understood?" Gears nodded grimly. The tech genius knew if required he'd have to fire even if they were still aboard an enemy ship when Nick signaled to fire.

"Bones, Kid, and Siren, meet me in the materializer bay in full body armor, armed with fully charged blasters and plasma rifles. Mehan, you still on the comm?"

"Yes, sir."

"Prepare a strike team to join us at the coordinates Gears will send you."

"Aye, sir."

Nick stood and led Bones, Siren, and the Kid to the lift. They were soon at the armory, gearing up for the mission ahead. Bones gazed silently at Nick. His eyes were intense and his body language revealed he was wondering something.

"Go ahead, Bones. What's bothering you?"

"Are we deploying the bio-weapon?"

"No," Nick said firmly. "We're too close to Earth." He slipped the sling for the plasma rifle over his head, then shoved a blaster into the holster hanging off his hips.

Bones forehead wrinkled. "Then what's the plan?"

Nick really didn't want to have this conversation. He'd been dreading it. "We're going to kill Bonetes." Siren, Bones, and the Kid stopped arming themselves and all eyes locked on Nick. "I know it's probably suicide to try, but taking off the head of the chicken is the only way to cause chaos among the enemy."

"Don't you mean head of the snake?" asked Siren.

Nick looked over his shoulder at Siren, his eyes wide with surprise. "How did you know that?"

Siren shrugged in a very human way. "I know all of your old Earth sayings, and I know the mistakes you make saying them."

"But you never said anything...I mean you never corrected me." Nick stammered. Siren shrugged again, her expression nonchalant. Nick relaxed and chuckled. "Well then, feel free to correct me anytime." Gears, Bones, and the Kid groaned.

Nick smiled to himself. These people were his family and he loved them even more at moments like this. Even the faux Siren had grown on him. Siren's clone wouldn't be ready for the mind transfer for at least two decades, so he was pleased this substitute for his second-in-command had complimented his crew as well as it had.

"Gears, are you and the *Thunder* ready to deploy the doodad ghost thing?"

Gears voice betrayed how annoyed he was by Nick's description of his sensor ghost technology when he replied. "Yes, sir, we're ready."

When they were within five thousand kilometers of the lead enemy battlewagon, the *Hunter* and the *Thunder* would project a fleet of five hundred copies of themselves to cause the enemy's short-range sensors to light up with enemy targets.

The enemy would overreact and hopefully begin targeting the false sensor images while the *Hunter* slipped inside their field of fire. Then both crews' assault teams would be transported aboard the battlewagon where they'd located Bonetes' biological signature.

After they were aboard, they'd locate Bonetes, kill him and anyone who tried to stop them. Once the madman was dead, they'd signal Grand Admiral Schipp, who would request the enemy's unconditional surrender or threaten that the Alliance Navy would destroy them.

Knowing Admiral Bellot Schipp and Alliance Council Chair Lokfor Ust, it was unlikely they'd actually ask the enemy commanders to surrender. The more likely scenario was the navy would attack during the confusion after Bonetes' death and kill every living being in the enemy fleet. The navy would then hunt down any enemy ships that managed to escape the carnage to kill their crews without mercy.

The Alliance would hire bounty hunters by the scores to scour the darkest corners of the galaxy until every possible threat to the Alliance posed by the remnants of the Master's followers was erad-icated from existence. They had to make an example of Bonetes and his minions so that no one would ever again threaten to wrest control from the corporations that ruled the galaxy with an iron grip.

Nick sighed to himself before ordering Gears to bring them to flank speed and bring the shields to maximum. "Prepare torpe-does and all cannons. Target their propulsion systems and concen-trate all initial fire on this area until they are disabled." No one responded since they were too busy and focused on the mission ahead.

The *Hunter* shuddered as blaster and plasma cannon fire raked their shields. "We have incoming plasma torpedoes. About a hundred or so," the SIN reported calmly.

"How many are tracking us?" asked Nick.

"All of them."

Nick cringed. The stealth shield had once again failed to hide their approach. Somehow Bonetes' techs had defeated their safe-guards every time. It made him wonder if there was another double agent among his crews.

"Is it possible to project a barrage of plasma torpedoes?" Nick grew excited by the possibilities, his stomach muscles tightening.

"No, unfortunately, I haven't had time to add that enhance-ment to the programming yet. But if we program our and the *Thunder*'s plasma torpedoes to make it appear they're coming from the ghost images, they might provide the distraction we need."

"Great idea, Gears, let's do it."

"We're firing every torpedo we have and so is the *Thunder*," reported the SIN. "They are being tracked by the enemy vessels and the false sensor images have appeared." The AI paused momentarily in its report. "The enemy is following the torpedoes back to the false sensor images."

Nick's excitement grew as it did during every mission. "Gears, take us in! And prepare to transport us aboard the target enemy ship." With a slight nod of his head, Siren, Bones, and the Kid followed him onto the materializer platform. They formed a circle, their backs to each other, their plasma rifles held at the ready.

Without warning, Nick felt the familiar tingling of the materializer beam being activated. The materializer bay around him became fuzzy, then disappeared. His next awareness of his surroundings, he was standing on a gleaming onyx-colored plasti-steel deck facing at least twenty or more heavily armed enemy troopers dressed head to toe in gleaming black blast armor. They had their visors up, revealing the scarred and stubble-covered features of hardened warriors preparing for combat. Their weapons were holstered or slung around their torsos.

Good, thought Nick, *we have the element of surprise.* He brought his plasma rifle to bear on two of the troopers and depressed the firing stud. A brilliant beam of concentrated plasma energy shot across the gap between them. The enemy troopers screamed in agony as the superheated plasma engulfed them, tearing the air from their lungs, boiling their blood, and roasting the flesh from their bones where the plasma met unprotected skin

Bones, Siren, and the Kid fired simultaneously and soon the twenty troopers lay dead on the deck, their corpses smoking, their body armor scarred with deep gashes revealing burnt flesh beneath. The smell of burnt ozone mingled with charred skin causing Nick's stomach to protest as his suit's filters were overwhelmed by the terrible stench of death all around them.

Siren had a hand scanner out and was intent on the screen. Nick forced his stomach to settle as he walked up to the comm unit recessed into the wall. They'd anticipated the weapons fire would attract unwanted attention. Sure enough, the comm unit buzzed.

Nick glanced at Bones, who was kneeling over one of the corpses. "Ripper, Japalp," he said.

Nick nodded, then pressed the comm unit's activation pad. "Ripper," he said keeping his voice low and menacing. Glancing at Bones, he saw the weapons specialist's brow was wrinkled and his eyes quizzical.

"We read a weapons discharge in your sector," said a cool feminine voice over the comm.

Nick released the reply activation pad. "Bones, what is it?"

"I know this guy," the big Martian said.

"Who is he?"

"A mercenary I knew many years ago from my home town on Mars."

The woman's voice was more urgent. "Ripper, report."

My accent is wrong. Nick realized. *The dead guy is Martian.* "Bones, you take over the comm."

Bones stood and hurried to the comm. He pressed the activation pad. "A trooper shot one of my team. We killed him," he said in perfect Martian. Nick glared at Bones, who shrugged. Bones' explanation might cause the person at the other end to dispatch more troopers to investigate.

"Okay. We're under fire right now. I'll notify the Legate, who will expect a full report when this is over."

"Will do," Bones said.

"Are you sure everything is okay down there?" the woman said.

"Why?"

"You should be addressing me as Prefect..."

Bones rolled his eyes. "Of course...my apologies, Prefect. We're all a little upset about our friend..."

The woman's voice became stern. "Fine for now, Centurion. But don't let it happen again. Loyalty in the chain of command is one of the Emperor's priorities."

"Yes, Prefect. All hail the Emperor." Bones released the activation pad.

Nick arched an eyebrow at his friend, and his lips formed an ironic smile. "Nice touch." His brow wrinkled. "But you took a hell of a risk with that explanation about the rogue shooter."

Bones shrugged and grinned. "I used to be a double agent, don't forget. I know how they operate. That Prefect won't be reporting anything to the Legate and I won't have to file a report."

The Kid chuckled. "You're not the real Ripper, so you'd never have to file the report regardless."

Gears caught Nick's eye. "Are these guys for real?" he whispered. Nick grinned.

"Bonetes' bio-signature is five decks above this one," said Siren, silencing the others.

"Okay," said Nick. "Which way to a lift?" Siren nodded toward the doorway leading to the corridor. Nick lowered his voice to a harsh whisper. "Follow me."

He led them into the corridor with Bones and the Kid last to cover the rear. As they hurried down the corridor, Siren indicated the correct direction with hands signals.

After what seemed like an eternity but in reality was no more than a minute, they arrived at a lift. The door slid open just as they arrived. Nick's heart leapt to his throat when he saw four heavily armed troopers inside. He fired his plasma rifle into the lift car, resulting in a cry of pain. The Kid came up from behind him to toss a grenade into the car.

"Fire in the hole," shouted the Kid before he landed on his belly and covered his head with his arms. Nick and Bones followed their friend's example.

Panicked yelling was suddenly cut short by a loud bang that shook the deck beneath them. Nick lifted his head and saw blood splattered across the wall beside the lift doors and acrid smoke billowed from inside the car. They certainly wouldn't be using that lift any time soon.

Nick rose to his feet and helped the Kid to his. "Nice job, Kid, but did you have to destroy the lift too?"

"Sorry, boss."

Nick looked to Siren, who hadn't dropped to the floor with the others. She looked exactly the same, unmarked by the explosion. "Siren, where's the next lift?"

"Twenty meters..." she pointed to the dimly lit corridor ahead. "That way, sir."

"Okay. But this time do you read any lifeforms?"

"None that I can detect," she said, her mouth a grim line as her gaze drifted over the bloody corpses in the damaged lift as the ventilating system cleared the smoke.

"Did you detect any in this lift before we got here?"

"No, sir, the walls in this section of corridor are difficult to penetrate with this hand sensing unit. The place we transported into was far easier. The deeper we go into the ship's interior..." She left off, the rest of her explanation unspoken.

"Gears, can you fix the problem?" Nick said over the comm to the tech genius who'd been monitoring their communications since they transported aboard.

"Give me a few seconds. I should be able to boost the scanner's range with a simple algorithm..." There was a short pause. "Okay, Siren, it should be good to go. Better?"

"Yes, much," she replied, surprise evident in her voice. "No, Captain, the lift ahead is unoccupied, but there are some twenty-seven enemy troopers headed to our coordinates from opposite directions." Before Nick could ask another question, she continued, "We will arrive ahead of them. If we hurry."

"Let's go. Quickly," Nick said.

They arrived at the lift and the doors were already open. Stepping inside, Nick studied the controls. They appeared to be secured by a high-security pad. It was impossible to tell what was needed to activate the lift.

"Gears, we're about to have a horde of unfriendlies for company. The lift has a security pad."

"Give me a second," Gears responded. The pad lit up. "Okay, Cap'n, close the doors. I'll lock them from here." Nick pressed the "door close" icon. The doors slid shut, but the lift car didn't move. He tried the icon for the deck they wanted, but still the lift didn't move.

"I'll have you moving soon, sir. It'll take a few minutes to bypass their internal security."

Nick sighed. "I guess we wait." He looked at Siren. "Where are the *Thunder*'s assault team right now?"

"They've made it to the target deck and hidden, awaiting our arrival." She paused briefly. "One of their number has been killed and another wounded."

"How do you know?" asked Bones.

"Gears programmed the scanner with different colored icons for our forces. Green means alive, yellow means wounded, and red means terminated. The enemy forces are all purple icons, either alive or dead," explained Siren, her eyes still focused on the screen.

"But how do you know they're hidden?" asked Nick, following Bones' lead.

"Their icons aren't moving and the enemy seems to be in static security positions. Neither grouping is near or approaching the other."

Nick arched an eyebrow at his second-in-command. "So you made an educated guess based on the data you had in front of you?"

Siren looked up from the screen, surprise registering on her narrow features. "Why, yes, sir, actually." Bones and the Kid snickered until Nick silenced them with a glare.

The lift began to move and the deck numbers on the control's screen showed they were rising. "Back to work, people. Everyone aim at the doors and prepare for enemy contact." Glancing at Siren, he saw her intense stare was locked on the screen of the hand scanner with her blaster in her other hand, her finger hovering above the activation stud. Nick's heart pounded hard and his arm muscles tensed.

The doors slid open to reveal a throne room much like the one he'd seen aboard the *Emperor's Blood*. He led his team out of the lift onto the black tile-covered deck, scanning for threats. Seeing none, he lowered his weapon.

"Siren?"

"The *Thunder*'s team is near the double doors to the left of the throne. There are forty of the enemy beyond those doors. Bonetes' bio-signature is among them."

Using hand signals, Nick led the way to the doors. Once there he nodded to the Kid, who stepped up and placed a wafer-thin device to the door on the right. A soft click in the silence told Nick it was magnetized and now affixed to the door.

"Everyone back," said the Kid. They stepped back a few paces, then the Kid pressed a small round object that had appeared in his left hand. There was a muffled explosion and the twin doors blew inward.

The Kid moved to the now open doors and tossed a grenade into the room beyond. A loud bang was followed by billowing smoke.

"Where is the *Thunder*'s team?" Nick asked Siren.

"Behind you, boss." Nick spun round to discover the grim features of Mehan Xsk, Captain of the *Thunder*.

"Let's go, then," Nick said simply. Both teams spread out, and once inside the room, blaster fire seemed to appear from every corner of the room. Nick's blast armor absorbed a shot and he stumbled under the force of the impact. He lifted his plasma rifle and activated the firing stud in the direction of the blast that struck him. He was rewarded by a scream of pain.

The air was hazy and there was a cacophony of screams as Blaster Squad took out Bonetes' guards. Finally the shooting stopped and the room quieted. Smoke drifted in the air, clouding Nick's vision. "Siren?"

'Yes, sir," came the immediate reply.

"Where's Bonetes?"

"He's about five paces to your left, sir. He has a weapon."

Nick turned to his left and fired the plasma rifle, keeping his finger on the firing stud, shifting the weapon back and forth to spray the area with super-heated energy. A sharp scream was followed by the thud of something heavy striking the deck.

Nick walked carefully toward where the sounds originated until he came across the charred remains of Asty Bonetes, trillionaire weapons dealer and would-be emperor of the galaxy.

The tension in Nick subsided and he lowered the rifle until the barrel pointed at the deck. "Gears, send the coded signal to Admiral Schipp. The Empire has fallen."

19

GSS Hunter
  Orbiting Earth
  Sol System
  4155.9.30 Galactic

NICK TOOK a sip of his cold coffee, then set the mug on his desk in his quarters. He stared at the screen in front of him. For the past month he'd been struggling to complete his after-action report required by Alliance Naval regulations.

He and his squad would still be part of the navy until he filed this report with fleet headquarters now that the crisis had ended. He relished the thought of once again being free of the Alliance Navy and all the baggage it carried.

The fleet was in bad shape. Twenty-three Alliance battlewagons and one hundred heavy cruisers had been destroyed, along with their crews; an undetermined number of destroyer class vessels and picket ships had yet to report in, presumed lost with all hands. The dead were numbered in the tens of thousands and rising.

Three of the large enemy battlewagons had been destroyed while the remaining three had been disabled and captured without firing their high-energy weapons at any planets in the Sol system. Thousands of the enemy's smaller vessels had been destroyed while the rest scattered after it was announced Bonetes was dead.

As Nick had anticipated, the remains of the Alliance fleet, along with their mercenary allies, were busy hunting down the enemy ships and showing no mercy in their execution of the enemy crews.

Nick thought of Jack Jameson, who was also killed in the fierce battle, recalling his wicked grin in their academy days after he'd pulled his latest prank on rookie cadets. Nick shook his head and smiled at the memory. Jack had been a good friend.

The faux Siren had been struck down, but the memory core remained undamaged. Siren's consciousness was safe and was being transferred to a new host body in the Bio-Medical lab in Sydney on Earth.

He froze as grief swelled in him. The Kid died in the firefight that killed Bonetes, and most of Mehan Xsk's crew had been killed or badly wounded. Some might still not make it but their consciousnesses would be transferred to new host bodies using the same process used for Siren. Unfortunately, the Kid had been hit in the head by a plasma blast and his brain was too damaged to attempt a recovery.

The price paid for victory was high. Maybe too high. He pushed away his grief and the feelings of regret as it occurred to him what would have happened if Bonetes had managed to conquer the Alliance. Better to deal with the devil you know than the one you don't, his grandfather used to tell him.

"SIN, I'm finished. Send the report to fleet headquarters along with Blaster Squad's notice of resignation from the navy."

"Yes, Captain."

The door chime sounded. "Come in," Nick said slumping in his seat.

Bones entered his quarters and the door slid shut behind him. "Hey, Cap'n." He moved to sit in the only other empty chair in Nick's cabin. "Report done?" Nick nodded.

Bones avoided looking at Nick by gazing at the desk. The monitor screen was now dark.

"What's next?"

Nick shrugged. "I'm done with this life, Bones. I just can't do it anymore."

"What's going to happen to the squad without you?" He leaned forward and placed a comforting hand on Nick's shoulder.

"When Siren's back on line, I'm transferring command of Blaster Squad to her. It's up to you and the others to select a new second-in-command, but I'd recommend Gears." He locked eyes with Bones. "No offense."

Bones offered his friend a wry smile as his hand dropped away from Nick's shoulder. "None taken. I like to keep busy shooting stuff. I'm not command material and we both know it."

Nick grunted in reply. "I'd also like you to take on a replacement for the Kid. An explosives expert, preferably." Bones eyes grew sad. It was Nick's turn to place a comforting hand on the weapons expert's shoulder. "You know I'm right."

Bones nodded.

Nick stood. "I'm headed to the bridge to check on the repairs underway." He grinned at Bones. "You never know what new tricks Gears has up his sleeves."

Bones smirked. "Yes, sir."

Nick led the way out his cabin door, his thoughts occupied by what he might do next with his life. Only time would tell.

. . .

To the reader: I hope you enjoyed these seven stories about Blaster Squad's battle with the Master. The squad will return when a new deadly threat engulfs the galaxy. So until then, set your blasters on stun and happy reading.

ABOUT THE AUTHOR

International selling Star Trek author, Russ Crossley, writes science fiction and fantasy, and mystery/suspense as well as their various subgenres.

His latest science fiction satire set in the far future, Revenge of the Lushites, is a sequel to Attack of the Lushites released in 2011. Both titles are available in e-book and trade paperback.

He has sold several short stories that have appeared in anthologies from various publishers including; WMG Publishing, Pocket Books, 53rd Street Publishing, and St. Martins Press.

He is a member of SF Canada and is past president of the Greater Vancouver Chapter of Romance Writers of America. He is also an alumni of the Oregon Coast Professional Fiction Writers Master Class taught by award winning author/editors, Kristine Katherine Rusch and Dean Wesley Smith.

Feel free to contact him on Facebook, Twitter, or his website http//:www.russcrossley.com. He loves to hear from readers.

OTHER TITLES BY RUSS CROSSLEY YOU MAY ENJOY

The Trudy Wilson Mystery Novel Series

Bad Loyalty

Shear Murder

Buzzcut - coming soon

Blaster Squad

#1 Terror on the Moon

#2 Sea of Death

#3 Planet of Doom

#4 Raiders of Cloud City

#5 Rise of the Empire

#6 Galaxy of Evil

#7 The Empire Strikes

Mercenary Knights – A Blaster Squad short story

Other Novels

Attack of the Lushites

Revenge of the Lushites

My Zombie Prince

Antique Virgin

The Fire In Their Hearts

with R.S. Meger (from Champagne Books)

Zomopolis

The Last Serial Killer

Razor and Edge Mysteries

The Kidnapping of Billy Buttons

String of Pearls

Death by Clown

Beggin' For Murder

Ragged Ice

The Grand Central Mystery

A Strange Case of Undead Murder

Jazz Stiletto Mysteries

A Day Without Sunshine

Skullduggery

Instrument of justice (first published in Over My Dead Body online
mystery magazine)

The Amanda Dark paranormal mysteries

Hook Island

Grind Manor

Moonrise Diner

A Father's Daughter

Dark Territory – Novel (coming soon)

Short Stories

Countdown

Shoeless Moe

Round Up At The Burger Bar:

The Story of Trixie Pug, Parts 1, 2, 3, 4, 5, 6, 7, 8, 9

Five Minutes

Blossom Queen, Barbarian

The Secret

The Family Line

End of the Flies

Death by Magic

The Penguin Sleeps With The Fishes

Only The Worthy

Hero For A Day

End of Empire

Strange Bedfellows

Big Business

A Perfect Crime

The Wise Guy and The Pirates

In Search of the Perfect Cup

T.I.N. Men

The Legend of G and the Dragonettes

The Incredible Mr. Fix-It

Lock Stock and Barrel

Divided Loyalties

Cave of Wonders

A Family Empire

Until We Meet Again

Dragon Rising

Solitary Man

The Keel Mountain Conspiracy

Angel on My Shoulder

Heroes of Old

The Great Bicycle Race

Tikka's Big Day

"My Partner the Zombie" —

Hungry For Your Love Anthology

(St. Martin's Press)

Big Hairy Deal

One Red Shoe

A Bad Day in Lunden Texas

Bloody Betty, Queen of the Pirates

Mirror Image

Dangerous Waters

Cape Disappointment

Boomerang

The Watcher of Wayburn Street

The Apprentice

Drip!

A Beautiful Friendship and The Parrot of Doom

Robine's Diary

The Christmas Club

Loose Ends

Splatter Pattern

It Takes Two

Lexicon

Replacement Parts

Sidekicks

Lost Stories

Time and Space

Survivors

Justice Served

Love Stories

Ladies of the Jolly Roger with Rita Schulz

The Adventures of Razor and Edge:

Five Tales From The Quirky Detective Team

An Unexpected Journey

On Edge

Thrilling Adventures

Total War

Courageous

Non-Fiction

The Writers Tools - The Synopsis

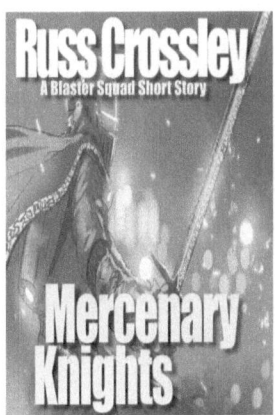